THERE WAS A STACK OF DRY WOOD INSIDE THE OLD HOUSE, AND JACE STARTED A FIRE . . .

"You could have any woman on earth. Why would you want an old maid like me?" Nellie said.

Jace pulled her into his arms and kissed her. "You were made to love and be loved."

His hands roamed over her body until Nellie wasn't sure she could breathe. He released her abruptly. "Look, ah, this is going to be a long night," he said. "Maybe we ought to eat something, then get a little sleep."

Nellie looked at him and knew what she wanted to do. She wanted him to make love to her.

She smiled at him, then moved the picnic basket nearer to the fire. As she looked inside it, she said, as though it meant nothing, "You'll catch your death in those wet clothes. You'd better remove them. You can wrap up in the lap robe."

Nellie was shaking as she withdrew food from the basket. She looked up at Jace slowly, up muscular calves to heavy thighs, then a small robe about his waist. The sight of Jace's broad, sculpted chest made her mouth dry.

"Oh my," she whispered. "My goodness, my." She had no idea an unclothed man could be so utterly, splendidly beautiful . . .

Books by Jude Deveraux

The Velvet Promise
Highland Velvet
Velvet Song
Velvet Angel
Sweetbriar
Counterfeit Lady
Lost Lady
River Lady
Twin of Ice
Twin of Fire
The Temptress
The Raider
The Princess
The Awakening
The Maiden
The Taming
A Knight in Shining Armor
Wishes
Mountain Laurel
The Conquest

Published by POCKET BOOKS

JUDE DEVERAUX

WISHES

POCKET BOOKS

New York   London   Toronto   Sydney   Tokyo   Singapore

This book is a work of fiction. Names, characters, places and incidents are either the product of the author's imagination or are used fictitiously. Any resemblance to actual events or locales or persons, living or dead, is entirely coincidental.

An *Original* Publication of POCKET BOOKS

POCKET BOOKS, a division of Simon & Schuster
1230 Avenue of the Americas, New York, NY 10020

ISBN: 0-671-74385-6

First Pocket Books printing November 1989

15   14   13   12   11   10   9   8   7   6

POCKET and colophon are registered trademarks of
Simon & Schuster.

Printed in the U.S.A.

Wishes

Chapter One

L ater, it was said that Berni was the best dressed corpse any of her set had seen in decades. Not that many of them admitted to having lived for much more than a couple of decades, and, what with the wonders of plastic surgery, none of them needed to admit to the exact number of years.

They filed by the expensive coffin and looked in admiration at Berni. There wasn't a line in her face. Every pit, wrinkle, even some of the pores had been shot full of collagen. Her breasts, filled with silicone, even in death pointed skyward. Hair expensively colored, eyelashes permanently dyed, nails manicured, waist tucked into a youthful twenty-three inches, her body clad in a six-thousand-dollar suit— she looked as good in death as she had in life.

There were sighs of admiration from the people attending, and hope that they would look as good in death as she did. Only two people shed any tears at Berni's demise, both of them men. One man was her hairdresser. He was going to miss Berni's business, but he was also going to miss Berni's wicked tongue and all the juicy gossip she passed his way. The other mourner was Berni's fourth ex-husband, and his tears were tears of joy, because he was no longer going to have to support the army of workers it took to keep a fifty-year-old looking twenty-seven.

"Going to the cemetery?" one woman asked another.

"I would like to, but I can't," said the second woman. "I have an appointment. Emergency, you know." Janine, her manicurist, could only give her a time slot today at two, and she *had* to have her broken nail repaired.

"Same here," said the first woman, and she gave a quick, guarded, angry glance at Berni in her coffin. Last week she'd bought the same suit Berni was being buried in, now she would have to return it. It was just like Berni to show up in the latest, the newest, the most expensive at *every* gathering. At least that won't happen anymore, she thought, and she managed to suppress her smile. "I do wish I could go. Berni and I were such good, close friends, you know." She smoothed her silk Geoffrey Beene pantsuit. "I really must leave."

Before long there were more murmurs of people having emergency appointments elsewhere, until, in the end, only Berni's hairdresser rode in the limousine to the grave. There was a line of twenty limos behind the hearse—Berni had arranged and paid for her funeral years in advance—but they were empty of mourners.

At long last the words (planned by Berni) had been spoken, the music (also planned by Berni) had been played and sung, and the single mourner had gone home. The grave was filled in, new sod rolled into place, flowers artistically arranged around the tasteful gravestone, and the sun began to set over Berni's grave.

Four hours after her coffin was covered, not one person gave a thought to the woman who had been so much a part of their lives. They had eaten her food, attended her parties, gossiped endlessly with her and about her, but no one missed her now that she was gone. No one at all.

THE KITCHEN

Berni opened her eyes with a jolt, feeling as though she'd overslept. Her first thought was that she'd be late for her nail appointment with Janine, and the bitch was ruthless if a client was late. She'd tell Berni she was booked up for the next week and make Berni suffer with ragged-looking nails for days. I'll get her, Berni thought. I'll tell Diane that Janine's been sleeping with her husband. With Diane's temper Janine will be lucky to come out alive.

Smiling, Berni started to get out of bed and then realized she wasn't in bed. It was then that she began to see that something was wrong. She wasn't in bed but standing up. She wasn't wearing her red silk Christian Dior nightgown but her new white Dupioni silk suit—the one Lois Simons had purchased on sale. Berni planned to wear the suit first, then Lois wouldn't be able to wear hers; she'd try to return it and wouldn't be allowed to, and she'd be stuck with a four-thousand-dollar suit she couldn't wear. The idea made Berni smile.

But she lost her smile as she looked around. There was fog everywhere, and she couldn't see anything except a gold-colored light far ahead. What now, she thought. She squinted a bit to see better, although she now had twenty-twenty vision thanks to eye surgery last year.

She took a few steps forward, and the fog cleared a path. She started to frown but caught herself (frowning gives one wrinkles). Perhaps this was some stupid idea of her latest lover. He was a twenty-year-old muscle-bound beachboy she'd picked up a few months ago, and she was growing tired of him. He kept talking about how he wanted to be a movie director, and he wanted Berni to finance him. Maybe all this fog was his doing to get her to open her checkbook.

She walked for several minutes before she saw anything. Under the golden light was a big desk, and behind it was sitting a handsome, gray-haired man.

When she saw the man Berni perked up and put her shoulders back so her high breasts pointed straight ahead.

"Hello," she said in her throatiest, sexiest voice.

The man glanced up at her then down at the papers on his desk.

It always worried Berni when men didn't immediately respond to her beauty. Maybe she'd better make another appointment with her surgeon next week. "Are you with Lance?" she asked, referring to her beachboy lover.

The man kept looking at his papers and didn't answer her, so Berni looked at his desk. She tried not to look startled, but his big desk was twenty-four-carat gold. Many years ago Berni had developed an eye for jewelry that would have made any jeweler proud. She could quickly and easily tell twelve-carat from eighteen-carat from the genuine, pure twenty-four-carat.

She reached out her hand to touch the desk but drew it back when the man looked up.

"Bernadina," he said.

Berni winced. She hadn't heard the name in years. It sounded as old as she fought not to be. "Berni," she said. "With an i."

She watched the man use an old-fashioned fountain pen to make a note, then she began to grow annoyed. "Look, I've had just about enough of this. If this is some scheme you and Lance have cooked up, I—"

"You're dead."

"—am still going to throw him out. I'm not going to support him, and—"

"Died in your sleep last night. Heart attack."

"—his harebrained schemes to—" She stopped and stared at the man. "I what?"

"Died in your sleep last night, and now you're in the Kitchen."

Berni stood there blinking at him, and then she began to laugh. She forgot about wrinkles and how unattractive a woman looked when she was laughing as opposed to smiling coyly and really laughed. "Great one, buster," she said, "but it won't work. I know this is a trick to get me to give Lance money, so you can turn off your fog machines and—"

She stopped because the man wasn't listening to her. He picked up a big stamp from the desk, smacked the paper with it, then motioned to his right. From out of the fog came a woman of about Berni's age—her *real* age, not how old she looked—wearing a long dress with lace at the elbows, looking as though she'd just stepped out of a play about Martha and George Washington.

Berni's only thought was that her beachboy had better be gone by the time she got back.

"Come with me," the woman said, and Berni followed her.

The fog still surrounded them, but it parted as they walked. After a while the woman stopped before what looked to be an arched doorway, again made of twenty-four-carat gold. Above the arch was a sign that said "Disbelief."

"I believe you need this," the woman said, stepping back.

Reluctantly, Berni entered the fog on the other side of the arch.

It was some time later that she left the room. Her eyes were no longer angry but were now filled with wonder and some fear. She had seen images of her death, her funeral, had even watched the undertakers embalming her body.

Outside the Disbelief room the woman was waiting for her.

"Better now?" the woman asked.

"Who are you?" Berni whispered. "Is this heaven or hell?"

The woman smiled. "I'm Pauline, and this is neither heaven nor hell. It's the Kitchen."

"The Kitchen? I just died, and I get sent to the *Kitchen?*" Her voice was rising in hysteria.

Pauline didn't seem in the least perturbed by her manner. "The Kitchen is a . . . I believe in your time you would call it a halfway house. It's between heaven and hell. It's for women only—not for bad women, not for good women—it's for women who don't quite deserve heaven or hell."

Berni just stood there gaping, her mouth open.

"It's a place for women who . . ." Pauline thought a moment. "For example, it's for all those religious women who spout Bible verses and consider themselves better than everyone else. They haven't been really bad, so to speak, so they can't be sent to hell, yet they've been so judgmental they can't really be sent directly to heaven."

"So they're sent here? To the Kitchen?" Berni whispered.

"Exactly."

Pauline didn't seem inclined to say any more, and Berni was still trying to recover from the news of her own death. "Nice dress," she managed to say at last. "Halston?"

Pauline smiled, either not understanding or ignoring Berni's bitchiness. "The women here are from all different time periods. You'll see every century from earth here. There are *lots* of Puritans here."

Berni felt her head reeling with all she'd learned. "Is there someplace to get a drink around here?"

"Oh, yes. What do you drink now? Bathtub gin, isn't it?"

"That was before my time," Berni said as they began walking, the fog clearing ahead of them.

"Whatever you drink, whatever you want, you'll find it here."

A moment later Pauline stopped in front of a tiny table, and on it was a tall, frosty margarita. Gratefully, Berni sat down and took a long drink as Pauline sat opposite her.

When Berni looked up, she said, "Why's this place called the Kitchen?"

"It's just a nickname. I'm sure it has another name,

but nobody remembers it. It's called the Kitchen because it's like women's life on earth. When you die you think you're going to heaven, just as you think, when you get married, that you're going to have heaven on earth. Instead, in both cases, you get sent to the Kitchen."

Berni nearly choked on her drink. She would have laughed, but instead her eyes widened in horror. "You don't mean I'm going to have to spend eternity cooking and . . . and cleaning out the refrigerator, do you?" Can a dead person commit suicide, she wondered.

"Oh, no, nothing like that. This place is very nice. *Very* nice. In fact, it's so nice many women never want to leave. They never do their assignments correctly, and they've been here for centuries."

"What assignments?" Berni asked suspiciously, still reeling with horror at the idea of years of cleaning floors and sinks and ovens and cooking a damned turkey every Thanksgiving.

"Every woman in the Kitchen is given, from time to time, a task to perform. She's to help someone on earth. The tasks are always different. Sometimes a woman is to help someone who's grieving, sometimes she's to help someone to make a decision. There are lots of different assignments. If you fail, you stay here."

"And if you succeed in helping the person, what do you get?"

"Eventually, heaven."

"Is heaven full of this fog?"

Pauline shrugged. "I have no idea. I've never been there, but I imagine it's better than this."

"All right," Berni said, standing, "lead me to my first task. I don't want to stay in a place even *named* the Kitchen."

Pauline stood, and the table, chairs, and empty glass disappeared. She started walking, Berni behind her.

Berni was thinking hard about what Pauline had told her. "Help someone on earth?" she muttered, then she stopped.

Pauline halted and looked back.

"Are we," Berni said, "are we fairy godmothers?"

"More or less," Pauline answered, smiling and starting to walk again.

Berni caught up with her. "You mean *I* am supposed to be someone's *fairy godmother?* Magic wands? Wishes and Cinderella and all that?"

"You're quite free to solve your assignment in any way that you see fit."

If Berni's collagen-padded face could have wrinkled into a frown, it would have done so. "I don't like this," she said. "I have my own life to lead. I don't want to be some fat, gray-haired lady running around saying 'Bibbidi Bobbidi Boo' and changing pumpkins into coaches."

Pauline blinked, not understanding Berni's allusion at all. "Leading your own life is what I imagine got you here instead of into heaven."

"What does that mean? I never hurt anyone in my life."

"Nor did you help anyone. You lived completely for yourself. Not even as a child did you ever consider anyone else's wishes. You married four men for their money, and when they complained you divorced them and took half of everything they owned."

"But that's how everyone lives in the twentieth century."

"Not everyone. You cared much more for clothes than you did for any of your husbands."

"The clothes gave me more pleasure," Berni said. "And besides, they got what they wanted. They weren't innocent in this. If they'd given me what I needed, I wouldn't have divorced them."

Pauline had no more to say. Having grown up in the eighteenth century, she didn't know that Berni's words were the product of years of expensive therapy. Berni only went to therapists who asked, "What do *you* want out of life?" "What do *you* need?" "What are *your* priorities?" Berni had always found someone to help her justify her belief that what she wanted was more important than what anyone else wanted.

With a little sigh, Pauline turned away and began walking again. "It looks like you may be here for a while," she said softly.

Berni followed her, thinking that Pauline sounded just like her four husbands. They were selfish through and through, always complaining that Berni never cared anything about them, that she only wanted them for what they could do for her.

Pauline stopped, and Berni halted also. Around them the fog began to clear, and she could see that they were standing in a circular room, very bare, and set in the walls were arches. Above the arches were signs: "Romance." "Fantasy." "Clothes." "Feasting." "Indolence." "Luxury." "Parties."

"Choose," Pauline said.

"Choose what?" Berni asked, turning about and reading the signs.

"You must wait while an assignment is found for you, and you will wait in one of the halls." Pauline could see that Berni still didn't understand. "What would you most like to do now?"

"Go to a party," Berni said without hesitation. Perhaps a loud, energetic party would get her mind off her own funeral and all the talk of ex-husbands.

Pauline turned toward the arch marked "Party," and Berni followed her. Once through the arch there was another fog-filled arch to the right. Above it was a sign: "Elizabethan."

Pauline stepped through the fog, and Berni saw a scene from Shakespeare. Men in capes, their legs in tight hose, were leading corseted women through the intricate moves of a sixteenth-century dance.

"Would you like to join them?" Pauline asked.

"This is *not* my idea of a party," Berni answered, appalled.

Pauline led her back through the arch and across the hall to another arch.

All in all they looked into half a dozen parties before Berni saw one that appealed to her. They saw a Regency party with women in muslin dresses sipping tea from saucers and talking about the latest escapade of Lady Caroline Lamb. There was a square dance with cowboys, a Victorian party with parlor games, a thirteenth-century feast with some fine-looking young acrobats that tempted Berni, a Japanese tea ceremony, and an amazing Tahitian dance, but in the end she chose a party from the sixties. The blaring music of the Stones, the bright mini dresses, the Nehru jackets, the smell of marijuana burning, the writhing bodies of the long-haired people reminded her of her youth.

"Yes," she whispered, and she stepped inside. In a moment she was wearing a micro-mini dress, her hair was long and straight, and there was a boy asking her to dance. She never looked back to see what had happened to Pauline.

Berni was huddled in a pile with other flower children, smoking grass and listening to Frank Zappa talk to Suzie Creamcheese when Pauline came for her. Berni looked up and knew she had to leave. Reluctantly, she left the party and followed Pauline out of the room.

Once they were through the golden archway the fog closed in over the room and hid all sights and sounds from them. Berni's beads and tie-dyed shirt disappeared along with her headband. Her head cleared of the effects of the marijuana, and she was once again wearing the silk suit in which she'd been buried.

"I just got here," Berni said sulkily. "I was just beginning to enjoy myself."

"By earth time you have been partying for fourteen years."

Berni could only blink at Pauline. Fourteen years? She felt as though she'd entered the party but moments before. She had been aware that now and then her clothes were different, but surely she couldn't have been in there fourteen years. She hadn't slept or eaten, had drunk very little, and hadn't had a single conversation with her fellow party-goers. She'd meant to talk to them about the Kitchen and about their assignments, but there had never seemed to be an opportunity.

"There is an assignment for you," Pauline said.

"Great," Berni said, smiling. If she passed this test and went to heaven, what pleasures awaited her there? Heaven must be some super place to be better than the Kitchen.

Pauline led them down a hallway, past several golden arches that Berni was dying to explore. One said "Harem Fantasy" above it, another "Pirates."

At last Pauline turned through an arch labeled "Viewing Room" and led them into a large room with a half circle of banquettes covered in peach-colored velvet. All around the seats was thick, white fog.

"Please make yourself comfortable."

Berni snuggled down into the soft, velvet-covered seat and looked where Pauline did, at the foggy wall in front of them. Within seconds the fog drew back and a scene appeared before them. It was like a movie, only not as flat, and like a play, only more real.

A young woman, slim, pretty, with light brown hair pulled back from her face, was standing before a full-length mirror. She was wearing a long dress with very large puffed sleeves. The dress was of dark green silk with sparkling black beads across the bosom, and it was so tight in the bodice it was a wonder she could breathe. There were three hatboxes on the floor, and the woman was trying on one hat after another. The room was pleasant, with a bed, a wardrobe, a dresser, a washstand, a rag rug, and a fireplace, but it certainly wasn't a palace. There were invitations open on the mantelpiece.

"I don't guess she can see us," Berni said.

"No, she has no idea anyone is watching her. Her name is Terel Grayson, she's twenty years old, it is 1896, and she lives in Chandler, Colorado."

"You mean I'm to make a Cinderella out of some antique girl? I don't know anything about history. I need someone from my own time."

"In the Kitchen all earth time is the same."

Berni looked back at the screen and sighed. "All right. So where's Prince Charming? And where's the wicked stepsister?"

Pauline didn't answer, so Berni watched in silence. Terel moved about the room quickly, looking at her invitations, then rummaging inside the big mahogany wardrobe. She sighed and looked disgusted as she pulled out one dress after another and flung them on the bed.

"That's just like me," Berni said, smiling. "I always had lots of invitations, and I was always worried about what I was going to wear. Not that I needed to worry, of course. I could have worn rags and been the belle of the ball."

"Yes," Pauline said softly, "Terel is like you."

"I could do something with her," Berni said. "A few cosmetics, soften her hair. She doesn't need much. She isn't as pretty as I was at her age, but she'll do. She has a lot of potential." She looked at Pauline. "So when do I start?"

"Ah," Pauline said, "here comes Nellie."

Berni looked back at the scene. The door opened, and in came another woman, older than Terel and about twice her size.

"Gross," Berni said, looking at Nellie. She had a slim woman's horror of obesity, and Berni's fear of fat was amplified by the fact that she'd spent most of her life starving herself in order to remain slim. Deep down she feared that if she made the least slip she'd be Nellie's size. "Two hundred pounds if she's an ounce."

"One hundred and sixty-two, actually," Pauline answered. "She's Terel's older sister, Nellie. She's twenty-eight, unmarried, and she takes care of Terel and their father. Their mother died when Terel was four and Nellie was twelve. After his wife died Charles Grayson had Nellie quit school and take care of the house and Terel. Nellie has been Terel's mother, so to speak, for most of Terel's life."

"I see," Berni said. "A wicked sister and mother combined. Poor Terel. No wonder she needs a fairy godmother to help her." She looked at Pauline. "Do I get a magic wand for this job?"

"If you would like. We can supply you with any magic you want, but you must supply the wisdom."

"That'll be easy. I'll see that Terel gets whatever she deserves, and I won't let that fat sister of hers keep her from getting the most out of life. Did you know that I have a fat older sister? She was so jealous of me, always trying to horn in on my life." Berni could feel the remembered anger rising in her. "My sister hated everything about me. She was so jealous that she would have done *anything* to make me miserable. I fixed her, though."

"What did you do?" Pauline asked softly.

"My first husband was her fiancé," Berni answered, smiling. "He really was the most boring man, but he had a little money, so I made him pay attention to me."

"You seduced him, didn't you?"

"More or less. But he needed seducing. My sister was—is—such a bore, and . . ." She looked at Pauline sharply. "Don't look at me like that. That man had more fun with me in the five years we were married than he would have had in a lifetime with my fat, dull, stupid sister. Besides, she turned out okay. She married and had a couple of fat kids. They were all quite happy in their middle-class way."

"I'm sure everyone was very happy. You most of all."

Berni wasn't sure she liked the woman's tone, but before she could reply Pauline said, "Shall we watch?"

Berni looked back at the scene before them, at the two women in the bedroom, and settled back to watch. She had to figure out how to help the slim, pretty Terel.

CHANDLER, COLORADO
1896

Nellie moved about the room, picking up Terel's clothes and hanging them back in the wardrobe. She also picked up the hats Terel had discarded and carefully put them back into the boxes.

"I cannot decide," Terel said petulantly. "Why do we have to live in this forsaken town anyway? Why couldn't we live in Denver or St. Louis or New York?"

"Father's business is here," Nellie said softly, straightening a feather on a hat. The hats weren't theirs but were on loan from the milliner. She was sorry they could afford only one hat and the others would have to be returned, but she meant to keep the ones Terel didn't want as clean as possible.

"Business!" Terel said, flopping down on the bed. "That's all anyone in this town talks of. Business! Why can't there be any society?"

Nellie straightened out another hat, stroking the dried hummingbird on the crown before she put it away in the box. "There was the very nice garden party at Mr. and Mrs. Mankin's last week, and the Harvest Ball will be at Mr. and Mrs. Taggert's."

Terel snorted. "All that lovely money and a family as crude as that. Everyone knows the Taggerts are little better than coal miners."

"They all seem very nice."

"Oh, Nellie, you think everyone is nice." Terel

propped herself on one elbow and watched her sister putting away clothes. Just last week, for the thousandth time, she'd heard someone say what an extraordinarily pretty face Nellie had, that it was too bad she was so heavy. Terel had even seen Marc Fenton watching Nellie. Marc was handsome and rich, and if he looked at anyone it should be at Terel.

Terel got off the bed and went to her dresser, opened a drawer, and withdrew a box of chocolates. "I have a gift for you, Nellie," she said.

Nellie turned and smiled at her beloved little sister. "You shouldn't give me things. I have everything I need."

Nellie's whole face lit when she smiled. Terel had heard women say that Nellie could light up a room with the warmth of her smile. "You wouldn't refuse my gift, would you?" Terel asked, lower lip extended in a pretty pout. She held out the box of chocolates, and Nellie's face fell. "You don't like it," Terel said, on the verge of tears.

"Yes, of course I do." Nellie took the chocolates. "It's just that I've been trying to eat less and lose some of this weight."

"You don't need to lose weight," Terel said. "You look beautiful to me."

Nellie's smile returned. "Thank you, dear. It's nice to have one person love me just as I am."

Terel put her slim arm around Nellie's plump shoulders. "Don't let anyone change you. You're beautiful just as you are, and the fact that men don't like you doesn't mean anything at all. What do they know? Father and I love you, and even if we're the only ones, that's all right. We love you enough to make up for all the men in the world."

Nellie suddenly felt very hungry. She didn't know why Terel's words of love should make her feel hungry, but quite often they did. It didn't make sense to her, but it seemed that love and food were mixed up together. Terel told her she loved her, and Nellie felt hungry.

"I believe I will have maybe just one piece of that candy," Nellie said, her hands trembling as she opened the box and jammed three pieces into her mouth at once.

Terel turned away and smiled. "What should I wear tonight?"

Nellie sneaked a fourth piece of candy. "What you have on is lovely," she said, swallowing. She was gaining control of her hunger.

"This hideous old thing? Nellie, I've worn this half a dozen times already. Everyone has seen it."

"Two times," Nellie said indulgently, putting the lid on the last hatbox. "And our guest tonight has never met you, so he can't have seen it."

"Nellie, really! You just don't understand how it is when you're an attractive woman, when you're young like I am and your whole life is ahead of you. Surely your youth wasn't *so* long ago that you can't remember."

Nellie was feeling hungry again. "Terel, I am not as old as you seem to think."

"Of course you're not *old,* you're just . . . well,

Nellie, I don't mean to be unkind, but you're just not on the market any longer. I am, and I need to look my very best."

Nellie ate four more pieces of candy.

At that moment there was a quick knock on the door, and the only servant in the Grayson household, Anna, appeared. Anna was young and strong, but sly, and she spent most of her limited intelligence trying to get out of work. Whenever Nellie complained that Anna didn't help her enough Charles Grayson said he couldn't afford a new maid or a second one and Nellie must make do.

"He's here," Anna said, her hair falling out of her cap.

"Who is?" Terel asked.

"The man that's come to dinner. He's here, and your father ain't."

"Isn't," Terel snapped. "What could the man be thinking of? He's an hour early, I'm not even dressed yet, and—Nellie, is dinner ready?"

"Yes," she answered. She'd spent the afternoon cooking, and now her dirty apron covered her dirty brown housedress. "Anna, show him into the parlor and tell him he'll have to wait until we're ready to receive him."

"Nellie!" Terel said, horrified. "You can't just let the man sit alone for an hour. Father would be furious. According to Father, the man saved his life, and now they're trying to do some business together. You can't just leave him."

"Terel, look at me. I'm dirty. I can't possibly receive

him. But you look beautiful, as always. You go to him, and as soon as I—"

"Me?" Terel said. "Me? But I have to change and do my hair. No, Nellie, you're the elder, you are our father's hostess. You go talk to the man, let me change, and when I'm dressed you can change. That's the only way it can be. Besides, what would *I* have to say to the old coot? You're so much better with old people than I am. You can have him hold your yarn or something. Father says he's a widower, so maybe you can talk to him about putting up jams or something. This is the way it *has* to be, Nellie, and I think you'll agree with me if you look at it unselfishly."

Once again, Nellie felt very, very hungry. She knew Terel was right. She *was* their father's hostess, and she was very good with people of her father's age, while Terel tended to yawn when in the company of older people. Nellie did not want to offend this man, as her father was trying to persuade him to manage his freight company.

"Tell him I will be down as soon as possible," Nellie said quietly to Anna. Nellie turned to leave the room, but Terel caught her.

"You aren't angry with me, are you?" Terel asked, hands on Nellie's shoulders. "It doesn't matter how you look, because everybody likes you. They'd like you even if you were the size of an elephant. Me, I always have to look my best. Please, Nellie, don't be angry with me. I couldn't bear it."

"No," Nellie said with a sigh, "I'm not angry with

you. Take your time changing and make yourself pretty. I'll take care of Father's guest."

Terel smiled and kissed her cheek. As Nellie started to leave the room she handed her the box of chocolates. "Don't forget these."

Nellie took the candy, and in the hall she stuffed six pieces into her mouth before removing her apron and starting down the stairs.

Inside her room Terel smiled and went to her wardrobe. Now, what to wear to dinner to meet her father's guest? As she looked the idea of changing clothes bored her. Nellie was right. What she had on was perfectly all right for dinner with some old man, a man who had come not to see her but to see her father. What did it matter what she wore? He was probably too old to see anyway.

She lifted the spread from her bed, put her hand under the mattress, and pulled out the romance novel she'd hidden there. If she didn't change, she'd have an hour or so to read before dinner.

Chapter Two

Nellie paused at the bottom of the stairs to take a quick look in the mirror on the wall. Her chestnut hair was straggling about her neck, there was a smudge of chocolate at the corner of her mouth, and there was a green stain—spinach, probably—on her collar. She didn't like to look down at her old brown cotton dress, for she knew the hem was soiled and there was a permanent stain on the skirt. Terel kept telling her she needed new clothes, had even offered to help her choose them, but Nellie never seemed to have time for clothes. What with cooking, and cleaning what Anna missed, and helping Terel manage her extensive social life, Nellie didn't seem to have much time for anything as frivolous as new clothes.

Now, on top of having to see to dinner yet, plus all

the instructions she had to give Anna to try to get her to be of some help in serving tonight, their guest was an hour early. Why, she wondered.

She walked into the parlor, and he was standing with his back to her, looking out the window. She knew right away that he wasn't an old man.

"Mr. Montgomery," she said, walking toward him.

He turned toward her, and Nellie nearly gasped. He was a *fine*-looking man. *Very* fine-looking. Terel was going to be happily surprised when she saw him.

"I'm so sorry to have kept you waiting. I—"

"Please don't apologize." He had a voice to go with his face and form. He was quite tall, slim, muscular, with dark hair and eyes. "I have been insufferably rude at appearing this early, and I . . ." He looked down at his hands.

Nellie had always had insight about people, somehow knowing what they needed. He's lonely, she thought, and she smiled. This very handsome man was just lonely. A handsome man come to call on her would have sent Nellie into a dither, but a lonely man, handsome or not, young or not, was something she knew how to handle. She forgot all about her dirty dress.

"We are pleased to have you, whatever time you arrive," Nellie said, and she smiled at him, that smile that transformed her already pretty face into one of beauty. She didn't notice that Mr. Montgomery's expression changed. He stopped looking at her in embarrassment for having arrived an hour early and started looking at her as a woman.

Had Nellie been aware of his change of expression she still would not have known what it meant. Handsome men looked at Terel, but not at her. She continued smiling. "We have a lovely garden," she said, "and it's much cooler there. Perhaps you'd like to see it."

"Very much," he said, returning her smile. There was a dimple in his right cheek.

She led him through the parlor, down the hall, and out the side door to the garden behind the house. The garden was one of Nellie's great pleasures. Her father thought that using any space for flowers was frivolous, but in this one matter Nellie insisted on having her own way.

The late fall sun was setting on the garden, and it was beautiful. Amid the tall corn grew marigolds, and chrysanthemums lived beside the cabbages. Poppies grew along the back fence, and in front of them were herbs that Nellie used in her cooking.

"Beautiful," he said, and Nellie smiled in pleasure. She rarely got to show off her garden. "Did you do this yourself?"

"A boy comes twice a week to help me weed, but I take care of it mostly myself."

"It is as lovely as its owner," he said, looking at her.

For a moment Nellie thought she was going to blush, but then she realized he was just being polite. "Would you like to sit down?" she asked, motioning to the little swing set up under the grape arbor. She hurried forward to remove the string beans she'd been breaking when Terel had called her to help with the hats.

"Yes, thank you," he said, taking the bowls from her. "You wouldn't mind if I helped, would you? It would make me feel at home."

"Of course not." She put the empty bowls between them—one for waste, one for the broken beans—and filled his lap with beans, then filled her own.

"Where is home, Mr. Montgomery?" she asked.

"Warbrooke, Maine," he answered, and once he started talking he didn't want to stop. He's as lonely as I am, Nellie thought, then she corrected herself. How could she be lonely when she had Terel and her father?

He told her of his life, of growing up near the ocean, of having spent as much of his life on a sailboat as on the ground.

"I met Julie when I was twenty-five," he said.

Nellie looked at him, at his profile, and she could see the sadness in his eyes, hear the grief in his voice. Her father had said Mr. Montgomery was a widower. "She was your wife?"

He looked at her, the pain in his eyes making her feel pain also. "Yes," he said softly. "She died in childbirth four years ago. I lost both her and the baby two days before my thirtieth birthday."

She reached across the bean bowls and clasped his hand. The touch seemed to startle him awake. He sat there blinking for a moment, then smiled. "I do believe, Miss Grayson, you've put a spell on me. I haven't talked about Julie since she . . ."

"It's the beans," she said brightly, not wanting him to be sad. "They're enchanted beans. Same ones Jack used to grow his beanstalk."

"No," he said, looking at her intently. "I believe it's you who has bewitched me."

Nellie felt herself blushing. "Mr. Montgomery, you are wicked, teasing an old maid like me."

He didn't laugh at her jest; his face grew serious again. "Who told you you're an old maid?"

Nellie felt very confused. "No one has to tell me. I . . ." She didn't know what to say. She'd never had such a divinely handsome man flirt with her before. Wait until he sees Terel, she thought. Terel, wearing one of her beautiful evening gowns, could bring a whole room full of handsome men to a halt. "My goodness, Mr. Montgomery, look what time it is. I have to finish dinner, and Father will be home soon, and Terel will be down, and I must change clothes and—"

"All right," he said, laughing. "I know when I'm being dismissed." He picked up the bowls, not allowing Nellie to carry them, and blocked her way on the path. "Tell me, Miss Grayson, are you as good a cook as you are beautiful?"

Nellie could feel her face turning brilliant red. "What a flirt you are, Mr. Montgomery. You'll have half the female population of Chandler blushing."

He took her hand in one of his and looked at it. "Actually," he said softly, "I don't flirt at all. In fact, I haven't looked at another woman since Julie died."

Nellie was speechless. Utterly without words. That this man, so handsome, a man to set any girl's heart on fire, would pay any attention to her, a fat old maid, was one thing, but that he acted as though she were the only woman he looked at was another.

She snatched her hand from his. "I am not a fool, Mr. Montgomery," she said. "You waste your soft words on me. Perhaps you should try tempting someone who is younger and more foolish than I am."

She had meant to set him on his ear, but all he did was smile at her, flashing that single dimple in his cheek. "It's good to know that I am a temptation," he said, dark eyes twinkling.

Nellie felt herself blushing again as she turned away and hurried toward the house, Mr. Montgomery close on her heels.

Inside the house all was chaos. Her father was home, and instead of finding what he'd expected—his two daughters entertaining his guest—he'd come home to an empty house. Anna had disappeared as usual, neither Terel nor Nellie could be found, and there was no sign of his honored guest.

Nellie, looking like the hired help, walked into the house, Mr. Montgomery behind her bearing bowls of string beans, just as Terel came down the stairs wearing not evening dress, as her father had requested, but an ordinary day dress. Charles Grayson's temper snapped.

"Look at you!" he said under his breath. "Look at the both of you! Nellie, I would fire a servant who dressed as badly as you. And have you been treating our guest as a *scullery maid?*" he asked, motioning to the bowls of beans.

Before Nellie could speak Mr. Montgomery put himself between her and her father, almost as though he meant to protect her. "Miss Grayson very kindly agreed to sit with me when I so rudely arrived quite early for dinner."

Nellie held her breath, for there was a hard tone to Mr. Montgomery's voice, as though he were almost daring her father. *No one* spoke to Charles Grayson in that tone.

Before her father could speak, before Mr. Montgomery could say another word, Terel came floating down the stairs, her eyes alight at the sight of the beautiful man.

"What is all the fuss?" Terel said in her best there's-a-handsome-man-in-the-room voice as she moved toward Mr. Montgomery. "Please forgive us, sir," she said, bowing her head demurely and looking up at him through her lashes. "We are usually not so inhospitable." Never taking her eyes from his face, she continued, "Shame on you, Nellie, for telling no one that Mr. Montgomery had arrived. If I had known, I would have hurried back from my charity work to entertain you myself. As it was, you can see that I had no time to dress properly. May I take those?"

Terel took the bowls from him and shoved them at Nellie. "Why didn't you tell me he was young and handsome?" she hissed. "Were you trying to keep him for yourself?"

Nellie didn't have a chance to answer before Terel slipped her arm through Mr. Montgomery's and began leading him toward the dining room.

Nellie turned away and went to the kitchen. So much for her afternoon's flirtation, she thought. So much for a handsome man's words that he wasn't a flirt. Even as Nellie told herself that this was what she'd expected, she suddenly felt very, very hungry, as hungry as she'd ever been in her life.

On the sideboard was the jam roly-poly she'd made for dessert. It was light sponge cake filled with home-made jam, then rolled into a log. Nellie didn't even think about what she was doing. She didn't bother with a plate, didn't bother getting a fork. One minute the dessert was there, and the next she had eaten it.

Afterward she stood staring at the empty plate, as much in wonder as anything.

Anna, found by Charles, came running into the kitchen. "They want dinner, and they want it now." The maid looked from the empty plate to Nellie's jam-smeared mouth and began to smirk. "You eat all the dessert again?"

Nellie looked away. She would *not* cry. "Go to the bakery," she said, trying to hold back tears of shame.

"It's closed," Anna answered, her tone of voice telling how she was enjoying her triumph.

"Go to the back. Tell them it's an emergency."

"Like last time?"

"Just go," Nellie said, almost pleading. She didn't want to be reminded of the other times she'd eaten the dessert meant for the family meal.

32

Her shame at once again having eaten an entire cake made her keep her head down throughout the meal. Anna lazily and sullenly served the dinner while Charles and Terel kept up a steady stream of conversation with Mr. Montgomery.

Nellie didn't enter into the talk because she was dreading the time when what she'd done would be discovered. Her father had specifically asked for jam roly-poly for tonight, and she knew he'd be angry when he didn't get it. She also knew he'd know instantly what had happened. Every word he'd ever said to her over the years about her eating came back to her. Throughout the long meal she prayed that her father wouldn't say anything in front of Mr. Montgomery.

All too soon, Anna brought in the bakery cake. There was silence from her father and Terel, and Nellie hung her head lower.

"Did it happen again, Nellie?" Charles Grayson asked.

Nellie gave a brief nod, and there was a longer silence.

"Anna," Charles said, "you will serve the cake, but I believe my eldest daughter has had enough."

"Nellie has a bit of a problem," Terel said in a stage whisper to Mr. Montgomery. "She often eats whole cakes and pies. One time she—"

"Excuse me," Nellie said as she tossed her napkin on the table and ran from the dining room. She didn't stop until she was outside in the coolness of the garden. For a while she stood there, trying to still her pounding heart, making all her usual promises to herself. She swore she'd try in the future to control her eating, she swore she'd try to lose weight. She promised herself all the things she'd promised her father during the many talks they'd had in his study.

"Why do you have to be an embarrassment to both me and your sister?" he'd said a hundred times. "Why can't you be someone we'd be *proud* of? We're afraid to go anywhere with you. We're afraid you'll have one of your attacks and eat half a dozen pies in front of everybody. We're—"

"Hello."

Nellie jumped at the sound of a voice. "Oh, Mr. Montgomery. I didn't see you. Are you looking for Terel?"

"No, I was looking for you. Actually, your family doesn't know I'm here. I told them I had to leave. I went out the front door and came through the back gate."

She couldn't bear to look at him in the moonlight. He was so tall and handsome, and she'd never felt so dirty and fat before in her life.

"It was a delicious dinner," he said.

"Thank you," she managed to mutter. "I must go in now. Would you like to see Terel?"

"No, I don't want to see your sister. Wait! Don't go. Please, Nellie, would you sit with me a while?"

She glanced up at him when he used her first name. "All right, Mr. Montgomery, I'll sit with you." She sat in the swing where they'd sat so companionably earlier in the day, but Nellie didn't say a word.

"What's there to do in Chandler?" he asked.

"Church socials, the park, riding, not much. We're a boring little town. Terel knows everyone, though, and she can introduce you."

"Will you go with me to the Harvest Ball at the Taggerts' in two weeks?"

She looked at him sharply. "Which Taggert?" she asked, stalling for time.

"Kane and his wife, Houston," he said, as though no other Taggerts were in town.

Nellie just sat there blinking. Kane Taggert was one of the richest men in America, and he lived in a magnificent house on a hill overlooking the town. His beautiful wife, Houston, gave elegant parties for their friends, and once a year they gave a magnificent ball. Last year she and Terel had been invited, Terel had gone while Nellie stayed home, but something had happened—she wasn't sure what—and this year they'd not received an invitation, much to Terel's horror.

"Terel would love to go," Nellie said. "She would love to—"

"I'm inviting you, not your sister."

Nellie had no idea what to say to the man. When she was twenty and much slimmer than she was now she'd had a few invitations from men, but she'd rarely been able to accept. At twenty she had had the responsibility of caring for her father and a twelve-year-old sister—and her father did not like his dinner late.

"Mr. Montgomery, I—"

"Jace."

"I beg your pardon."

"My name is Jace."

"I couldn't possibly call you by your Christian name, Mr. Montgomery. I have just met you."

"If you go with me to the ball, you'll get to know me better."

"I couldn't possibly. I must . . ." She couldn't think of a single reason why she couldn't go, but she knew it was an impossibility.

"I'll take the job your father is offering if you'll go with me. And if you'll call me Jace."

Nellie knew that her father wanted this man to take the job, knew that he needed someone to help run his freight company, but none of this made sense. Why was he trying to persuade her to go somewhere with him? "I . . . I don't know, Mr. Montgomery. I don't know if my father can spare me. And Terel needs—"

"What that young lady needs is . . ." He didn't finish his sentence. "I won't take the job unless you agree to go with me. One evening, that's all I ask."

Nellie imagined entering the big white house on the hill on the arm of this extraordinarily handsome man, and she quite suddenly very much wanted to go. Just once she'd like to go out for an evening. "All right," she whispered.

He smiled at her as he stood, and even in the darkness she could see his dimple. "Good," he said. "I'm very pleased. I'll be looking forward to it. Wear something beautiful."

"I don't have anything . . ." She didn't finish. "I will look forward to the evening also," she whispered.

He smiled again, put his hands in his pockets, and, whistling, left the garden.

Nellie sat where she was for a moment. What an extraordinary man, she thought. What a very unusual man.

She leaned back in the swing, smelling the sweet fragrance of the flowers. She was going to the ball with a man. And not just any man. Not the butcher's fat son Terel was always suggesting, or the grocer's seventeen-year-old son who sometimes looked at Nellie with big eyes, and not the sixty-year-old man her father had once introduced her to. Not the—

"Nellie! Where have you been?" Terel demanded, standing over her in the darkness. "We have been looking all over for you. Anna is destroying the kitchen, and Father wants you to watch her, and I need you to unlace my dress. We're suffering while you sit here daydreaming. Sometimes, Nellie, I don't think you care about anyone but yourself."

"Yes, you're right. I'm sorry. I'll straighten out Anna." Reluctantly she left the swing and the garden and went back to the very real world inside the house.

It was hours later that she got the kitchen straight, had listened to another of her father's lectures about her eating, and was finally able to get to Terel's room.

"I got Anna to undo my laces," Terel said bitterly, sitting in her robe and gown before her mirror and brushing her hair.

Nellie began to pick up Terel's clothes. She was very tired and longed to take a bath and go to bed.

"Wasn't he divine?" Terel said.

"Who?"

"Mr. Montgomery, of course. Oh, Nellie, aren't you ever aware of anything that goes on?"

"He was very nice, yes."

"Nice? He was much more than nice. I've never seen a better-looking man in my life, except maybe Dr. Westfield, but he's taken. Father says he thinks there's money in his background."

"I think Dr. Westfield is quite comfortable," Nellie said tiredly.

"Not Dr. Westfield! Nellie, why don't you listen sometimes? Father thinks Mr. Montgomery has money. I can't imagine why he'd consider a job with Father if he has money unless . . ."

"Unless what?"

"Well . . . I hate to say it myself, but did you see the way he looked at me during dinner?"

Nellie, behind the wardrobe door, was glad Terel couldn't see her face. "No, I'm afraid I didn't see, but Terel, dear, you must be used to men looking at you."

"Yes," she said softly, looking at herself in the mirror. Mr. Montgomery had indeed looked at her, but not in the way men often looked at her. In fact, there was something almost chilling about the way he'd looked at her with those almost-black eyes of his.

She put her hand to her throat. He would be a challenge to win, she thought.

"I wonder what his name is," Terel murmured.

"Jace," Nellie said before she thought.

Terel looked at her sister in the mirror. Nellie was standing so that just her face was visible above the little screen by the washstand. In the candlelight Nellie was beautiful. Her skin was flawless, her lashes long, her lips full. Glancing back at her own reflection, Terel knew she wasn't half as pretty as Nellie. Next to Nellie, Terel's face was too long, her nose too sharp, and her skin wasn't nearly as smooth.

Terel opened a drawer to her dresser and withdrew a little bag of caramels, then went to Nellie and put her arm around her. "I'm sorry Father was such a beast at dinner. He didn't have to tell Mr. Montgomery about how you'd eaten all the cake. You weren't looking, but you should have seen the look on that man's face."

Nellie moved away from Terel's embrace.

"Nellie, I'm sorry. I didn't mean to offend you. I thought you'd be able to see the humor in the situation. It is amusing that a woman could eat an entire cake by herself."

"It is not amusing to me," Nellie said stiffly.

"All right, I'll stop laughing if you can't. Really, Nellie, if you'd just learn to laugh sometimes you'd have a much easier time in life. Where are you going?"

"To take a bath and go to bed."

"You're angry."

"No, I'm not."

"Yes, you are, I can tell. You're angry at *me* because of what Father said. That isn't fair at all. I'd never tell a guest I had a sister who could eat a whole cake."

Nellie could feel herself begin to grow hungry.

"I have a present for you," Terel said, holding out the bag of caramels.

Nellie didn't want the candy, but every time she thought of that handsome Mr. Montgomery knowing the truth about her she felt a hunger pang. "Thank you," Nellie murmured, taking the bag, leaving the room, and eating half the candy before she got to the bathroom.

THE KITCHEN

The fog closed over the scene, and Pauline turned to Berni.

"So that's my assignment?" Berni said thoughtfully. "I think I can handle it. What a hunk that guy Montgomery is. If I were there, I'd want him myself. Does he have money? It would be nice if he had money, because then he could buy Terel some more clothes. She could have—"

"Your assignment is Nellie."

"He could buy her a mansion or, better yet, build her one. He could—what?"

"Your assignment is to help Nellie."

Berni was too stunned to speak. "What help does she need? She has everything. She has a family who loves her and—"

"Does her family love her?"

"They must. They put up with her. You saw her eat

that cake. Disgusting. I wouldn't live with someone like that."

"Even if that person cooked and cleaned for you and picked up your clothes?"

"I see. This is all meant to make me feel sorry for the fat girl. No one opened her mouth and forced that food inside her. *She* ate that cake. She eats candy all day long. No one makes her."

"Mmm," Pauline said.

Berni got off the banquette. She was growing angry now. "You're just like those bleeding hearts on earth, always talking about eating disorders and how people can't help themselves. Do you think I stayed slim all my life because I'm naturally thin? I'm thin because I *starved* myself. I got on my scale every day, and if I was so much as a half pound heavy, I fasted that day. *That's* how a person keeps from getting fat. Discipline!"

"I don't think Nellie is as strong as you. Some people, like you, can make it through life all by themselves, but people like Nellie need help."

"She has help. She has a family that puts up with her. There she is, a fat old maid, yet her father's supporting her."

"He certainly seems to be getting his money's worth."

Berni glared at Pauline. "You think you know this fatty, but you don't. I know what fatsos like her are *really* like. She looks like she's the model daughter, taking care of her father and sister, acting reluctant when a gorgeous man asks her out. She may look like the perfect angel, but underneath all the blubber beats a heart full of hatred. I know."

"You know Nellie that well?" Pauline asked softly.

"I know women just like her. My sister is fat, and she *hated* me. She hated the way the boys asked me out, the way everyone looked at me and no one ever looked at her. I tell you, if you could see the true nature of this Nellie, you wouldn't see some meek little earth mother, you'd see a demon."

"That's difficult to believe."

"I know what I'm talking about. Every fat girl who ever saw me wanted to look like me. They all hated me because they were jealous—just as Nellie is jealous of that lovely Terel."

"You're sure Nellie actually hates her sister?"

"Positive. If Nellie were given what she *really* wants, Terel's arms would probably drop off. She would . . ." Berni stopped. "What do I have to do to help this Nellie?"

"It's up to you. I told you, we supply the magic, and you supply the wisdom."

"Wisdom," Berni said, smiling. "I don't know who chooses these assignments, but they goofed this time. Nellie doesn't need help, it's Terel who needs the help. I could prove it if I could give Nellie what she really, truly wants."

"You can."

Berni thought about that. "All right, I'll give her three wishes. Not dumb wishes like 'I wish the dishes were washed' but wishes for what Nellie genuinely wants. She doesn't have to voice her wish, just want it, you know what I mean?"

"I believe so. You think that what Nellie seems to want and what she really wants are at odds?"

"Odds? Are you kidding? Little Miss Goody Two Shoes will wish that hunk belonged to her, and she'll wish Terel into an early grave. You mark my words. I'll return, and Terel will be scrubbing floors. She'll probably wish her father into the poorhouse."

"Return?" Pauline asked. "You mean to give her three wishes and walk away? You don't plan to stay and see what happens?"

"I like that Terel; she reminds me of myself, and I can't bear to stay and watch what her fat sister is going to do to her."

"You're sure Nellie's heart is full of hatred?"

"*Very* sure. I know my fatties. Now, what do I have to do to give her her three wishes?"

Pauline sighed. "Declare it, nothing more."

"Okay, fatso, you get three wishes for what you *really* want. Sorry, Terel." Berni waved her hand in the direction of the screen. "Now," she said to Pauline, "what other rooms are in this burg? How about the Luxury room?"

Pauline gave a backward glance at the screen, sighed, then led Berni through the archway toward the hall.

Chapter Three

CHANDLER, COLORADO
1896

Jace Montgomery dismounted his horse, threw the reins to the boy waiting outside the Taggert mansion, and went inside. The butler didn't even rise from his chair but kept reading his paper, only glancing up to nod in Jace's direction.

"In his office?" Jace asked.

The butler nodded again and kept reading.

Jace knew the man didn't consider him a guest. In the butler's opinion there were guests and there were relatives, and Jace was a mere relative. As Jace walked through the big, mostly marble house the place rang with the sound of people, and the noise made him smile. The house sounded so much like his home in Maine.

His father's big, very old, sprawling house, set but

feet from the ocean in Warbrooke, Maine, always echoed with the noise of his Montgomery and Taggert relatives, and in the background was the constant music made by his mother and her friends.

After his wife died Jace couldn't bear the happiness around him. He couldn't stand to hear children laughing or see couples looking at each other with love. A month after he buried Julie and his three-day-old son he'd stepped on a train, and for four years he'd been traveling, just traveling, doing nothing else. He had met few people, not wanting ever again to care for another human being, and he'd kept to himself.

But about six months ago he'd started to recover, started to be able to think of something besides his own grief. He went to California and visited his mother's parents and spent some time with the old mountain men who lived on his grandfather's ranch.

It was while he was visiting Grandpa Jeff that his Aunt Ardis started writing him and nagging him to visit his Taggert cousins in Colorado. He gave in when he found out his cousin, Kane Taggert, and his wife were going to be in San Francisco. Jace took a train south and introduced himself. He found Kane to be as gruff-voiced and as generous-hearted as the Taggerts in Maine, and they became quick friends. Jace also fell half in love with Kane's beautiful wife, Houston.

The Taggerts had returned to Colorado, Jace had gone back north to spend a few more weeks with his grandparents, then he'd started the journey to Colorado.

He'd taken his time traveling, and it was at one

remote stop that he'd met Charles Grayson. During a sleepless night Jace had looked out the window to see a couple of thugs trying to rob a man. Jace was off the train in seconds, and a couple of well-placed fists easily dispersed the thieves.

Charles had been very grateful, and once on the train he'd started saying he needed a man like Jace to work for him. Jace didn't bother saying he didn't need a job or want one; he just listened to Charles talk about himself and his beautiful daughter. When Jace found out Charles lived in Chandler, he decided to visit the Grayson family and so accepted a dinner invitation.

Once in Chandler Jace had quite suddenly become very homesick, and, knowing Charles was at his freight office, he'd gone to the Grayson house an hour too early for dinner. He wanted to see this daughter Charles said was such a paragon of grace and beauty.

Within ten minutes of meeting Nellie he agreed with everything Charles had to say about her. She was kind and warm and funny, and for the first time in four years he found himself talking about his wife's death. It had been so pleasant to sit in the garden with her and break beans. She hadn't been flirtatious like so many women were. Instead, she'd blushed like a schoolgirl, and that beautiful face of hers had made him feel better than he had in years.

It was with disbelief and no little horror that he'd heard Charles Grayson cursing Nellie when they'd returned to the house. For a moment Jace had been too stunned to react. Charles had talked of nothing else on the train except his lovely daughter, yet here he was acting as though he were ashamed of her.

Still confused, Jace had sat through a long, boring dinner in which Nellie didn't say a word but her sister never stopped talking. It took Jace some time to realize that when Charles spoke of his daughter, he meant the younger one. As far as Jace could remember, Charles had never even mentioned that he had two daughters.

By the end of the meal, Jace began to understand what was going on. It seemed that both Charles and his younger daughter thought Nellie was *fat*. Jace looked at her, and indeed there was a bit more of her than there was of some women, but she didn't look like more than he could handle.

He looked at the younger sister, the one who was supposed to be so talented and so beautiful, and all he heard was the word *I*. Terel seemed interested only in herself, and she assumed that others were interested, too.

The meal seemed to go on forever, and he could hardly wait to get away from Charles and his vain daughter. He'd escaped as soon as he could and gone through the back gate. He'd guessed correctly that Nellie would go to her garden. Being alone with her in the garden was as pleasant as he remembered. Before he knew what he was doing, he'd agreed to work for Charles—a man of whom his opinion was now much lower—if Nellie would go to the Harvest Ball with him.

He smiled now as he walked into Kane's study. He meant to get more out of Nellie than a couple of dances.

Kane was bent over his big desk with his friend and partner, Edan Nylund, a man nearly as big as Kane but as blond as Kane was dark. Playing on the floor, tumbling about like puppies and making as much noise as a couple of steam engines, were three children ranging in age from one to three. Two were dark, one blond, so Jace guessed that two of them belonged to Kane and one to Edan, but he couldn't tell the sex of the children.

"Hello," Jace shouted over the noise of the children.

Kane looked up. "What brings you here?"

"I've come to run away with your wife." He nodded a greeting to Edan.

"Good," Kane said. "Make sure she takes those damned kids with her. Quiet down, all of you!" he yelled, but the kids ignored him.

A moment later all three children hushed, and Jace looked toward the doorway. Houston stood there, as beautiful, as serene as he remembered. "Children," she said, "leave your fathers alone. Go and find Uncle Ian." Obediently, the children left the room, the oldest holding the youngest's hand.

"Now," she said, smiling, "what can we do for you, Jocelyn?"

Jace winced, and behind him Kane snorted. Only his mother called him by his real name, and during his lifetime he'd bloodied several noses when anyone else called him Jocelyn. But Houston had called him Jocelyn since they'd met, and when they were alone he didn't mind.

"I really just came to visit," he said, but Houston stood and looked at him. He was years older than she, but she had a way of making him feel like a child. He cleared his throat.

Behind him Kane laughed. "You might as well tell her. If she says you came here for a reason, then you probably did."

Jace smiled. "All right, I'm caught. Houston, could I see you privately?" He looked at Kane. "I have a proposition to make to you."

"She gets propositioned often enough by me to keep this house full of kids," Kane said, more than a little pride in his voice.

Houston acted as though she were ignoring her husband's words, but there was a faint blush under her skin. "Come with me," she said, and she led Jace into a small, pretty, quiet sitting room.

"How is your visit to Chandler?" she asked when they were seated. "Meet anyone interesting?"

Jace laughed. "I hope it's not that apparent to everyone."

"When we met you in San Francisco you were so miserable there was a gray tinge to your skin. There is a bit of a sparkle in your eyes now, and if I'm not mistaken, you look as though you're up to something."

"I am," he said with a slow, lazy smile. It was a smile not many women had seen, and those who had, had said yes. "I am going courting."

Houston swallowed. She was happily married, but she wasn't dead. "I am sure you will win any woman you choose."

"I mean to, but I may need your help." Jace stood and walked to the window. "What do you know of the Grayson family?"

"Not a great deal. He's a widower with two daughters. They've only lived in Chandler for a few years, and I'm afraid I haven't had as much time to welcome newcomers as I once did. Two babies in four years has kept me busy."

"Yes, I can imagine it would." He looked back at her. "Have you invited them to your Harvest Ball?"

"Kane"—she hesitated—"Kane asked me not to invite them."

"Don't tell me *you* don't like Nellie?"

"Nellie? Nellie is a dear. She is the most generous person in the world, always ready to help anyone who needs her, but last year two young men engaged in fisticuffs in the garden in a battle over the younger daughter's favor. Kane said—well, he said some unpleasant things about the character of the younger daughter, so an invitation was not sent to the Grayson family this year. I fear that some young man will bring her, though." She looked up sharply. "You are not one of her suitors, are you?"

Jace smiled. "It's Nellie who interests me."

Houston looked at him for a long while. She had not spent much time with Nellie, but she'd always thought men were fools not to see beyond her thick figure. Men fell all over themselves over that vain, frivolous Terel, but not one man so much as asked Nellie to a church social. Yet here was Kane's cousin, this very good-looking man, saying he was interested in Nellie. Her opinion of Jace, already high, rose several degrees.

"I will issue an invitation to Nellie at once. Is there anything else I can do?"

"I don't know much about this sort of thing, but I don't believe Nellie has a dress to wear. Could you . . . ?"

"Of course," Houston said, her opinion of Jace rising even higher. "Don't you think Nellie would look splendid in silver? Silver and pearls?"

"I think Nellie would look splendid in anything." He took Houston's hand and kissed it. "You're a real lady, you know that?" He didn't know why Houston laughed so hard, but he was glad he'd pleased her.

Nellie was feeling frazzled. During the two days since Mr. Montgomery's visit she had been trying to make up to her family for embarrassing them. She had cooked some magnificent meals—of which she had eaten very little—and she had doubled her energies in cleaning. She and Anna had taken the front parlor's curtains down, hauled them into the backyard, and spent hours beating the dust out of them. In the evenings she'd been very tired, but she'd still stayed up late embroidering the lapels of a jacket she was making Terel for Christmas.

She hoped that if she was good enough, her family would forgive her for making a fool of herself, and them, in front of a guest. She really did want to make her father and sister proud of her.

Now she was up to her elbows in flour as she rolled out dough for an apple pie for dinner. She had already prepared a standing rib roast, even cutting the little paper frills for the rib tops. Everything was ready to be put in the oven for dinner tonight.

She was so absorbed in the pie that she jumped when someone knocked on the frame of the back door. The door was open, since—with the stove filled with wood and blazing—the kitchen was hot.

"I knocked at the front, but no one answered," Jace said, smiling at Nellie and clutching a large bouquet of late fall roses.

"I'm so sorry," Nellie said, putting her rolling pin down and wiping some of the dough off her arms. "Anna is supposed to be dusting, but I guess . . ." She trailed off, remembering her father's lectures about telling family business to outsiders. She looked at the flowers and smiled. "I guess you've come to see Terel, but I'm afraid you've missed her. She—"

"I came to see you." Without being asked, he stepped inside the overly warm kitchen. "For you," he said, holding out the roses.

Nellie stopped where she was and blinked at him. She didn't take the flowers.

Jace walked to the table, took a slice of apple from

the bowl, and ate it. "You don't like roses? I thought you did, but if you don't I'll get you something else. What do your other beaux bring you?"

Nellie was tempted to look behind her to see if there was someone else in the kitchen to whom he was talking. "I like roses," she whispered, "and I have no . . . male friends."

"Good," he said, and he smiled at her warmly.

Nellie couldn't move but just stood there watching him as he sat on the edge of the table eating apple slices.

"You want to put them in water?"

"What?"

"The roses," he said, smiling again.

"Oh. Oh, yes." She recovered a bit as she took the roses from him. The Grayson household owned several vases to accommodate the many bouquets of flowers Terel received, but Nellie had never received so much as a daisy before. She slowly arranged the flowers, taking her time so her head could clear. Calm once again, she turned back to him.

"Thank you for the flowers, Mr. Montgomery, but I'm afraid Terel won't return for hours yet. She—"

"I want you to take a walk with me."

"Walk? You mean walk to where Terel is? I'm sure—"

"I do *not* want to see your little sister," he said sternly. "Nellie, I came to see you and no one else. I want you to walk with me."

Nellie took two steps backward. "I couldn't possibly do that. I have much too much work to do. I have to finish my pie, the roast has to go in the oven soon, I have to dress for dinner, and—"

"One hour," he said. "That's all the time I'm asking of you."

"It's not possible." Nellie backed away from him even further. She didn't care for the way he was looking at her. He was making her feel uncomfortable. "I have much too much to do."

"Thirty minutes then. Thirty minutes of your time for a lonely stranger in town. Walk with me downtown and introduce me to people."

"I don't know many people," she said quickly, "and I have to finish my pie. I couldn't possibly—"

"An apple pie?"

"Yes. It's for dinner. My father loves apple pie. He—"

"How can you make an apple pie without apples?"

She looked at him, then at the bowl that had a moment before been filled with apple slices. "Mr. Montgomery!" she said, sounding like a schoolteacher, "you have eaten the entire pie!"

"An easy thing for a person to do," he said slowly, watching her.

Nellie knew instantly that he was referring to her having eaten all of the dessert the night he came to dinner. Blood rushed to her face as she remembered her shame, but then she looked at him. His eyes were twinkling, and that dimple showed in his cheek. He was *teasing* her.

Her embarrassment left her, and she smiled at him, that warm smile that transformed her into a beauty.

"It seems to be very easy for *me*," she said, laughing. "Now what am I going to serve for dinner? We have no more apples."

His eyes were dancing. "I guess you'll have to walk to the store and buy more."

"So it seems."

"Maybe I should walk along with you, just in case of danger."

"Yes, perhaps you should. The streets of Chandler can be quite dangerous. Why, only last year two boys on bicycles ran into each other."

"No! That's horrifying! Who knows when something like that might happen again? I definitely think you need an escort."

"I rather think I do, too," Nellie said softly. Part of her mind was telling her to say no, that she should stay home and finish cooking. She should dismiss this overly familiar man and get on with her work. She was sure it wasn't at all proper for him to saunter into the kitchen as he'd done. But there was another part of her mind that told her to go. It would be very pleasant to walk with this handsome man and say hello to people. Maybe, just for this one afternoon, she could pretend that she was like other young women and a handsome young man had come to call on her.

She removed her apron and hung it on a hook by the door. She should probably go upstairs and get a hat, should probably look at herself in a mirror, but she was afraid that if she left him alone he might disappear. She didn't have Terel's confidence that even if she kept a man waiting for hours, he'd be there when she showed up.

She turned to Jace and smiled. "I'm ready."

He smiled back. He was very pleased that she didn't spend an hour or so primping before a mirror before she'd leave the house. It was his experience that women as beautiful as Nellie gave much time and thought to adorning themselves.

He stepped aside so she could walk in front of him through the door, and he admired the gentle sway of her hips. A bit of hair straggled about her neck, and he had an urge to lift it and kiss her fine skin.

"I'm sorry, I didn't hear you," Jace said when he realized Nellie was speaking. He'd opened the gate for her, and they were on the boardwalk.

"I forgot my basket." She turned back to the house.

He couldn't bear to let her out of his sight, and he was afraid that if she went back to the house he'd never get her out again. "I'll carry all your purchases." He couldn't help himself. He reached out and lifted the little tendril of hair, his fingertips lingering on her neck. Her skin was as fine and as warm as he'd imagined.

Nellie was startled when he touched her, and then embarrassed. Was her hair such a mess? Of course it was. After dusting, weeding, cooking, and washing, she knew she had to look dreadful.

"I must—" she began, then she stepped back quickly.

She stepped right into Miss Emily, a tall, thin, very

proper older woman who ran Miss Emily's Tea Shop. Miss Emily's packages went scattering about the boardwalk.

"I'm so sorry," Nellie began, angry at herself for seeming never to do anything right. She stooped and started gathering packages.

Miss Emily remained standing and looked down at the two young people gathering her packages. She could have let the shop deliver her purchases for her, but she found that when a woman of her age walked about town carrying bundles some very interesting things happened.

"Well, Nellie," Miss Emily said when they were standing. The young man was holding her packages and beaming at Nellie as though he were the cat that had eaten the cream. "Aren't you going to introduce me to your young man?"

"Mr. Montgomery isn't . . . I mean, we aren't . . ." Nellie stammered, flushing.

Jace grinned, making Miss Emily blink. He was a splendid-looking young man. "I may not be yet, but I mean to be her young man," he said slowly. "I'm Jace Montgomery."

"Emily," she answered, "or Miss Emily, if you prefer." She gave a hard, shrewd look at Jace. "I must say, young man, that you look pleased with yourself."

"I am." He looked at Nellie, whose face was still pink. "What man wouldn't be when escorting such a beautiful woman?"

Nellie again felt like looking behind her to see

whom he meant, but she could see that he was smiling down at her.

"Well, well, well," Miss Emily said. "At last there's a man in this town with some sense. Nellie is a *fine* young woman, quite, quite fine, and you'll do very well to hang on to her."

Jace took Nellie's hand and slipped her arm through his. "I think I might do that," he said, smiling at Miss Emily.

"Come to my shop for tea," Miss Emily said.

"I'm sorry, but I have to return home and—"

"We'll be there," Jace said as Miss Emily took her packages and started walking.

Jace began walking in the opposite direction, Nellie's arm held securely in his.

"Mr. Montgomery," Nellie began, "you really can't say things like that."

"Say things like what?"

"That I . . . I am beautiful, and that you are my young man. You will give people the wrong impression about us."

It never crossed Jace's mind that Nellie didn't *know* she was beautiful. It was his experience that beautiful women often complained about their lack of looks, and he knew that when they did, it was because they wanted compliments. He wasn't ready to yet give extravagant compliments to Nellie. He wanted his hands to be on her body when he told her how beautiful she was. "What would be the right impression about us?"

"That you work for my father, and that, as his hostess, I feel I should . . ." Should what, she thought. She'd never gone walking with any of her father's other employees.

"Should introduce me to the citizenry of Chandler," he finished for her. "Which is why I think we should go to Miss Emily's shop." Abruptly, he stopped and looked down at her. His face was quite serious, as he'd just had an awful thought. "You don't dislike me, do you, Nellie? Maybe you'd rather not be seen with me. Maybe I'm not—well—appealing to you."

Nellie could only look up at him; she was capable of saying nothing. Dislike him? Unappealing? He was the most handsome man she'd ever seen in her life. He was kind, thoughtful, warm, funny, and charming. "I like you," she whispered.

"Good." He tucked her arm in his more securely and started walking again. "Now, tell me about this town."

Nellie tried to relax somewhat, but it was difficult. She didn't understand him because he was different from any man she'd ever met. Most men looked her up and down then ignored her. A few men had shown some interest in her, but it was usually for her cooking and her housekeeping skills. Four years ago a widower with five children had asked her father for Nellie's hand in marriage. Nellie would have married him— she would love to have children—but Charles and Terel had been so upset that Nellie had turned the man down. Her father and Terel had said the man only wanted to use her to take care of his children, that he didn't really care for Nellie and she should wait for the "right" man to come along. Nellie hadn't been foolish enough to believe the man loved her, and she had known that, at twenty-four, she didn't have too many chances for marriage left, but she had given in to her father and Terel and refused the man's proposal.

Afterward, she had eaten so much that she'd gained twenty pounds. Her father didn't say a word about her weight gain, but Nellie often felt his eyes on her. She seemed to disappoint him in every way possible. She was a burden to him, an unmarried daughter, and even when she had found a man to marry he was quite unsuitable.

One day Terel brought home the news that the man who had asked Nellie to marry him had married someone else and bought the big old Farnon house on the river. Terel softened the news with a gift of a four-pound box of chocolate fudge—all of which Nellie ate in an afternoon.

"And what is that building?" Jace asked.

They were walking down Lead Avenue toward downtown Chandler, and she began to point out shops and businesses to him. They went past the Denver Hotel, Farrell's Hardware, Mr. Bagly's tailor shop, and Freyer Drugs, then took a left on Third Street and kept walking.

After a while Nellie began to get over her nervousness, for Jace was easy company. He seemed to be interested in everything, wanting to know how old buildings were, who owned what, what was for sale.

"You sound as if you might be considering living here permanently."

"I might," he said, looking down at her in a way that made Nellie turn away.

On Coal, in front of Sayles Art Rooms, Johnny Bowen and Bob Jenkins saw Nellie and came running.

"Is Terel with you?"

"Is she at home?"

"Could I see her later?"

"What are you serving for dinner?" Bob asked, laughing.

Nellie felt herself coming back to earth. For the last hour, basking in the glow of Jace's warm eyes, she'd forgotten all about her beautiful young sister. "She's—" Nellie began.

"If you will excuse us," Jace said sternly, looking down his nose at the young men, *"Nellie* and I have a previous engagement."

The young men were so astonished they couldn't speak for a moment. "You that new guy working for Terel's father?"

"For Mr. Grayson, yes," Jace said pointedly.

Bob grinned. "Oh, I see, the boss's daughter. Nellie—"

Jace dropped Nellie's arm and stepped toward the young men. Jace was older, larger, and much more self-confident. "I doubt, sir," he said, "if you have the intelligence to see anything. Now, I advise you to scurry along, and do not again mistake Miss Grayson for her sister's social secretary."

The men looked from Jace to Nellie and back again. Johnny, in the back, looked at Nellie as though seeing her for the first time in his life. He looked at her, not as Terel's fat older sister who quietly served tea and cakes and long, glorious dinners, but as a woman. He'd never noticed what a pretty face she had. And although she was too big for his taste, she did have a nice shape.

Johnny punched Bob on the arm. "We're sorry to have bothered you, sir. Good day to you, Nellie." He tipped his hat, and both men turned away, but Johnny glanced back over his shoulder at Nellie.

"Insolent pups!" Jace muttered, clasping Nellie's hand and curving her fingers about his arm. This entire town seemed to be full of lunatics, he thought. Were all the men blind, or just stupid? It was beyond his understanding how any man could be interested in that pinched-face, skinny-flanked, self-centered Terel when Nellie was in the vicinity.

At the corner of Second and Coal they could see Miss Emily's Tea Shop. "I'm hungry, are you?" Jace asked.

Nellie was still reeling from the encounter with Terel's young men. Mr. Montgomery had acted as though he were about to strike the men, and he'd said Nellie wasn't Terel's "social secretary." "No," she answered honestly, "I'm not hungry at all." She felt too good, too happy to be hungry. She wasn't aware of it, but her shoulders were straight, and there was a light in her face that hadn't been there an hour ago.

"Do you mind if I eat?"

She looked up at him. At the moment she would allow him *anything.* "Of course not," she said softly.

Inside the tea shop Nellie's shoulders sagged, for there were three of Terel's lovely, thin girlfriends. All three wore exquisite dresses and jackets that were as tight as sausage casings on their perfect, willowy figures. Their little waists looked as if they might snap in two.

"I think I should return home," Nellie whispered, acutely aware of her old house dress, of her straggling hair, and, most of all, of her size. She couldn't bear to see Mr. Montgomery's reaction when he saw the lovely creatures.

One of the girls looked up, saw Nellie, gave the tiniest smile in greeting—after all, she'd eaten at Nellie's house many times—then looked at her companions. But the next moment she looked back and looked up at Jace. For a second the girl lost her composure as her mouth dropped open.

Nellie looked away as Jace escorted her to a table. She took a seat and looked out the window. She didn't want to see Jace's face when he saw the pretty girls.

"Nellie, how wonderful to see you!"

Slowly, she turned away from the window to look at the girls standing by their table. They looked like a bouquet of flowers in their lace-trimmed gowns, snippets of fur on their jackets, jewels in their ears, saucy little hats perched on their pretty heads.

She knew what they wanted: to be introduced to Jace. She took a breath. Better to get it over with. "May I introduce you?" she asked softly. She introduced them, but she still couldn't bear to look at Jace, to see the way he looked at them. One of the girls slipped off her gloves, and Nellie could see the lovely way she moved her little hands.

Vaguely, she could hear Jace and the girls talking, but she wasn't really listening. It had been a wonderful afternoon, being on the arm of this man and pretending that he was hers.

"Will you excuse us?" she heard Jace say. "Nellie and I are hungry."

Nellie prayed for the floor to open and swallow her. People her size pretended they never ate.

"Oh," one of the girls said, looking curiously at Nellie.

"Mr. Montgomery, are you the man Terel said is going to work for her father?"

Nellie at last stole a glance at Jace and, instead of the enraptured expression she expected to see, she saw annoyance.

"I have agreed to work for *Nellie's father,*" he said emphatically, "only on the condition that Nellie walk out with me."

Nellie didn't know which of them was more stunned, herself or the three girls. In unison they turned to look at Nellie, and their expressions showed that they had no idea why a man like Jace would want a woman like Nellie.

Silently, they floated back to their table, and instantly their pretty heads were bent together as they looked at each other, then at Nellie, and back again.

Turning toward Jace, Nellie was once again speechless.

"This is the strangest town I have ever seen," Jace said, partly in anger, partly in puzzlement. "You'd think no one had ever seen a man and woman walking out together before. Is Colorado so very different from Maine?"

She started to tell him that the difference was not in states, but in women. What people found odd was that he wanted to be seen with Nellie. But something told her to be quiet. If he didn't know she was an undesirable, dried-up old maid, she wasn't going to be the one to tell him. He'd find out soon enough, so why end it sooner than need be?

"Perhaps Colorado is different from Maine," she said. "Tell me more about Maine and your boats."

"Gladly," he said, smiling, for he missed the sea.

Chapter Four

After a lovely tea, of which Nellie ate very little, they went back outside.

"I must go home," Nellie said, not meaning it. At the moment she felt as though she never wanted to go home again.

"You would look pretty in that," Jace said, looking in the window of the store next door, Chandler's largest, most expensive department store, The Famous.

Nellie never gave much thought to her clothes. She was too busy taking care of the house and cooking, and if she did have time off, she helped Reverend Mr. Thomas with charity work. Now, looking at the lovely clothes in the window, she did wish she had something pretty to wear.

"Like to go inside?" Jace urged.

"No," she answered, backing away. She couldn't bear all those slim, smug shopgirls, and the idea of purchasing a dress made her fear jinxing the day. "No, I must go home. Father will—"

Jace pulled out his big, gold pocket watch and looked at it. "Imagine that. We have been gone only ten minutes. Plenty of time yet."

"Ten . . ." Nellie began, then laughed. "All right, Mr. Montgomery, it looks as if we have another fifty minutes. Where shall we go?"

He slipped her hand in the crook of his arm. "Anywhere I am with you, I seem to be happy."

Nellie blushed, but she also felt a warm pleasure spread through her. "Fenton Park isn't far away," she lied, knowing it was half a mile. She'd worry about the rib roast and the unmade apple pie later.

They walked slowly, Nellie relaxing more with each step. Jace was very courteous to her, and he didn't desert Nellie as she feared he would.

At the end of Second Street Nellie halted. Fenton Park was in front of them, but between them and the park was a four-foot-high stone wall and then a deep ditch. "I meant to go down First Street," Nellie mumbled, feeling stupid. "We'll have to go back."

"What's a little wall? I'll lift you up, and you can climb over."

Nellie felt like laughing at him. Did he also think he could lift houses? Draft horses?

"Too undignified?" he asked, looking at her face.

She might as well say it. "Mr. Montgomery, three men couldn't lift me over that wall."

One minute she was on the ground, and the next he had his hands about her waist and she was being lifted. Jace was very strong from many years of hauling anchors and lashing down sails, and Nellie wasn't even especially heavy to him.

Nellie did laugh when she was on top of the wall. What a day, she thought, what an incredible, unbelievable day! No standing over a hot stove or hanging wash; instead she was walking with a divine man who treated her as though she were beautiful.

She stood on top of the wall and began to walk along the rim, her hands out for balance. Her childhood had ended one day when she was twelve years old, on the day her mother had died. For sixteen years there had been no foolishness, no wasted hours in her life.

Jace stood back and watched her walking on the wall. She seemed to grow younger and happier by the minute. He made a leap, and in a moment he was on the wall with her, and when he held out his hand to her she took it. "If we fall, we go together," he said, liking the idea of tumbling down the ditch together. "This way."

Nellie, holding his hand, followed him south along the wall toward Midnight Lake. A gust of wind came and she almost fell, but he caught her in his arms and pulled her close to him. Nellie had never been held by a man, and she could feel her heart pounding.

With one swift movement Jace pulled the pins from her hair and threw them away. Nellie's long, chestnut hair flowed to her shoulders.

"Beautiful," he whispered, and he put his cheek next to hers.

Nellie thought perhaps her body might stop functioning.

He pulled away, his face inches from hers. "I'd kiss you, but we seem to have an audience."

Nellie looked across the ditch to the park to see half a dozen young couples playing croquet, only now they had paused to look at Nellie and Jace on top of the wall. "Take me away before I die of embarrassment," she whispered.

"Your wish is my command."

For a flash Nellie thought of what her father would say when he heard of this, but she pushed the thought from her mind. *Now* was all that mattered.

Jace got down first and then lifted his arms to help Nellie down. She had a moment of doubt that he could hold her, but she was beginning to trust him. He took her weight easily, and for a moment he held her to him.

"People are watching," she said, pushing him away while blushing and laughing.

He took her hand and began to run with her, down one side of the ditch and up the other, then through the trees east of the lake, then further until they were at the edge of the park. Jace stopped, Nellie beside him, her heart pounding from the run, and looked out across the rolling countryside to the mountains. In the distance was a train, and they could hear its faraway whistle.

I'm falling in love, Jace thought. Falling in love with this woman who looks at me as though I'm twenty feet tall. She looked at him through her thick lashes, and he felt as though he could do anything. Julie had looked at him like that. And when he was married to Julie he *could* do anything. And since her death he had been able to do nothing.

But now, with every minute he spent with Nellie he was feeling more alive.

Nellie was trying to tie up her hair, but she had no pins or string.

"Leave it down," he said, looking at her and wanting to touch her, but it was too soon yet. He knew he needed to go slowly with Nellie. And he was willing to go as slowly as needed.

"All right," Nellie said softly, and she put her hands at her sides.

He led her up a little hill, then pulled her down to sit beside him, and when Nellie was seated he turned and put his head in her lap. Nellie was, for a moment, too shocked to respond.

"Mr. Montgomery," she at last managed to whisper, "I don't think . . ." She trailed off. Somehow, in the lessening afternoon light, it seemed right that this heavenly man should rest his head in her lap. The whole afternoon had been magical, and this was just part of the magic. Tomorrow she would be back to cooking and cleaning, but today she was going to participate in the magic.

He closed his eyes, and, tentatively, she put her fingertips to his temple to touch the soft hair there. He didn't open his eyes but gave just a bit of a smile, enough to make the dimple in his cheek show. She ran her finger along that dimple.

"Did you get your dimple from your father or your mother?" she asked softly. For this moment she could pretend she was like any other young woman and this man was hers.

"Father's family," he said, not opening his eyes. "Montgomerys now and then have dimples, and sometimes the girls get red hair."

"And your mother's family? What are they like?"

Jace smiled as Nellie's hand softly stroked his hair. "Talented. All the Worths are reeking with talent. My mother sings, her sister paints, my grandfather sings, my grandmother and her father paint."

"And what do you do?" Nellie was growing more bold as he lay there, his eyes closed. When Terel was small Nellie had held her and cuddled her, but as Terel grew older she'd wanted to be independent and hadn't allowed Nellie to mother her. Today Nellie was beginning to remember how pleasant it was to touch another human being. She ran her fingers through his hair, feeling it curl as she mussed it. She touched his eyebrows, his chin, felt the whiskers just under the surface of his skin.

"A little of both," Jace said, his voice husky. It was difficult for him to remain quietly in her lap, difficult not to take her in his arms. Not yet, Montgomery, he told himself, not yet.

"My mother tried to teach me to sing," he said, "but I never had the discipline. I'd rather be on a boat. My grandmother taught me some about drawing, and I was able to use that to design a few boats for my father's company, but mostly I just did what I could."

Nellie suspected he was being modest. Just as she'd sensed his loneliness when she'd first met him, she now knew he was not telling her all the truth. "No doubt your father paid you a salary in spite of the fact that you are a wastrel."

His eyes flew open. "I earned my keep. In fact, I designed a yacht that outran everything on the eastern seaboard. Neither of my brothers could design a rowboat, and I have some medals at home that—" He broke off, then grinned and settled back in her lap. "I'll owe you for that, Nellie," he said, smiling. She'd made him act like a bragging schoolboy. He picked up her hand and kissed the palm. "Now tell me about you."

"There's nothing to tell," she said honestly. "I have no talents, no accomplishments." Except eating, she thought. One day she ate three whole cakes.

"Music?"

"No."

"Art?"

"No."

"You can cook."

"So can a great many women."

He opened his eyes and frowned up at her. "You're not telling me the truth. There must be something you like more than anything in the world."

"I love my family," she said dutifully, but when he kept frowning at her she sighed. "Children. I've sometimes thought I'd like to have a dozen children."

"I would love to help you," Jace said solemnly.

It took Nellie a moment before she understood what he meant, then she blushed furiously and pushed at his shoulder. "Mr. Montgomery, you are wicked!"

He leered at her, wiggling his eyebrows. "You make me feel wicked, Nellie."

She laughed. The sun was setting, and the day was growing dim. She didn't know how it was possible, but he was even better-looking in the fading light.

"Listen," he said.

There was a church at the north end of the park, and in the stillness they could hear a Christmas carol.

"Choir practice," Nellie whispered. "For the services on Christmas Eve."

"Christmas," Jace said softly. "Last Christmas I don't even remember where I was, but I got drunk and stayed that way for two days."

"Because of your wife?"

Jace sat up and looked at Nellie, looked at her lovely face, then put his hand on her cheek, then touched her hair. He looked down at her body, at her big breasts, her waist over hips that he'd like to put his hands on. He wondered if her thighs were as white as the skin on her neck.

It suddenly occurred to him that he hadn't had a woman since Julie. In the four years of his wandering no woman had appealed to him. When he'd looked at women, all he saw was Julie, and every woman paled in comparison to her. But now, looking at Nellie, he wanted her so much that he found his hand was trembling.

"Let's go listen to the music," he said at last. He had to get her away from the quiet solitude of the park or he didn't know if he could control himself.

Nellie had no idea what was going on in his mind, but she knew she didn't want to leave the park. No man had ever looked at her as he just had, and although it frightened her, it also excited her. She was sure that today was a one-time event and that tomorrow there would be no strolls with a handsome man, so today she had to take all that she could.

"Nellie, don't look at me like that. I'm only human, and a man can take only so much."

She hesitated.

Jace rocked back on his heels and groaned.

The groan made Nellie laugh. She wasn't sure what was going on, but the look on his face made her feel powerful—and beautiful. "All right, let's go listen to the carols."

He helped her stand, and it seemed that his hands were all over her body at once. Nellie's heart leapt to her throat; her blood pounded in her temples.

"Let's go," Jace said, grabbing her hand and pulling her forward.

The pretty little white church stood out against the dark sky. The double doors were open, and golden lantern light spilled out into the cool night air. Jace put his arm around Nellie, and when she shivered he led her inside the church. They stood at the back and watched and listened as the choir leader took the men and women through Christmas carol after carol. Some of the choir members smiled at Nellie and looked in question at Jace, who stood protectively near her.

Nellie leaned against the back wall of the church and knew she'd never felt so good in her life. Her clothes brushed against his and, behind the cover of her skirt, he slipped his fingers into hers and squeezed.

They listened to the lovely music for some time, content just to be near each other, fingers entwined, and to do no more than listen.

It was when the choir leader directed the singers to change from carols to hymns that Nellie felt Jace stiffen.

"What is it?" she whispered.

"We have to go," he said urgently.

Some instinct told her that under no circumstances should they leave the church. She tightened her grip on his hand and said, as though to an unruly child, "We must stay."

Jace didn't move but stayed where he was, and Nellie tried to figure out what had upset him so. The choir began to sing "Amazing Grace," and at the first notes she felt Jace's hand in hers begin to tremble.

The choir had just begun to sing when Jace dropped Nellie's hand and stepped forward into the center of the church aisle. Nellie watched as he closed his eyes and began to sing the hymn. He had a beautiful, rich tenor voice, and the perfection of his tone showed his years of training. One by one the choir members stopped singing and listened.

Jace didn't hear the words he sang; he felt them.

The last time he'd sung the song was at Julie's funeral. He'd stood over her grave, dry-eyed, bareheaded in the frigid cold of Maine in February, and felt nothing. He felt neither the cold nor his deep sorrow. He imagined his pretty little wife in her coffin, their tiny son wrapped in her arms, and he'd felt nothing.

He had sung the song, and while others had wept he had shed not a tear. For four years now he had felt nothing, had moved, had eaten, had slept, but he had felt nothing. For four years he had not laughed or cried or even been angry.

Now, as he sang the old, mournful words of the hymn, he remembered Julie, remembered her laughing, remembered her as she struggled to give birth to their child.

It was time to say goodbye to the woman he had loved so much. At long, long last tears came to his eyes. Goodbye, my Julie, he thought. Goodbye.

When Jace stopped singing, the stillness inside the church was profound. No one even breathed—and there was not a dry eye in the building. They had felt the emotion in Jace's words and responded to it.

At last someone blew his nose, and the spell was broken.

"Sir," the choir leader said, "we'd like you to sing in our choir. We'd—"

Nellie hurried forward. "We'll talk about it later," she said with finality, and she half pushed Jace out the door. Outside he leaned against the church wall, and Nellie took his handkerchief from his pocket (hers was dirty) and gave it to him.

Jace blew his nose loudly, then gave a weak smile to Nellie. "Not much of a way for a man to act in front of his girl, is it?" he mumbled.

His words made Nellie's heart flutter, but she controlled herself. "Your wife?"

He nodded. "I sang that at her funeral."

"You loved her very much?"

He was recovering himself and realized that for the first time since her death Julie wasn't quite as clear to him as she had been. He looked at Nellie, and it was her features he saw instead of Julie's. "Loved," he said, emphasizing the past tense. "Yes, I did." He put his hand on Nellie's cheek. "Could I walk you home, Miss Grayson?"

"Home?" she asked, as though she'd never heard the word before. Then suddenly, like fire drenched by water, she came back to reality. "What time is it? Oh, don't tell me. Father will be frantic. They'll not have had their dinner. Oh, no, what have I done?"

"Something for yourself, for a change," Jace said, but Nellie was already running west toward her house. He ran after her.

While Nellie and Jace were in the park, Terel was entering Dr. Westfield's clinic. She was beautifully dressed in a suit of dark plum, the tight-fitting jacket covered with black braid sewn on in an intricate design.

The only other person in the office was Mary Alice Pendergast, a thin-nosed young woman some years older than Terel. In Terel's mind, Mary Alice was an old maid just like Nellie, and therefore not any competition nor worthy of much attention.

She greeted Mary Alice and took a seat.

"I find Dr. Westfield so much more competent than a female doctor, don't you?" Mary Alice said, referring to the women's clinic run by Dr. Westfield's wife.

"Much," Terel agreed. "I wouldn't trust a female, especially with something as serious as my heart palpitations."

"Mmm," Mary Alice said, agreeing. "And Dr. Westfield is so handsome, don't you agree?"

"That has nothing to do with it," Terel snapped, looking away. Dr. Westfield was, in her opinion, the best-looking man she'd ever seen—until Mr. Montgomery arrived in town, that is. Truthfully, it would be hard to choose between the men.

Since Mr. Montgomery had come to dinner Terel had done some checking on him. It seemed that he had some money; she wasn't sure how much, but her sources whispered that he wasn't poor. He was a relative of that vulgar Kane Taggert, and that man was certainly wealthy enough.

For a while Terel had puzzled over why Mr. Montgomery had taken a job with her father. Why didn't he work for his rich cousin? It was when she remembered the way he'd looked at her at dinner that she understood. Mr. Montgomery had, no doubt, taken her father's job to be near Terel. Terel was used to men looking at her, but Mr. Montgomery had looked at her differently—so differently that she'd felt herself flushing a few times.

Of course, he was the first *man* who'd looked at her; all the others had been mere boys.

She'd spent today with her dressmaker. It was her opinion that a new wardrobe never hurt when embarking on a new venture. And her new venture was the pursuit of one Mr. Montgomery. He was comfortably well off, if not rich; handsome; and, from the looks of things, he was mad for Terel. Of course, his connections to the rich Taggerts helped. She would be a cousin by marriage, and never again could the Taggerts deny her entrance to that big house of theirs. Perhaps after she married Mr. Montgomery they could live in the house with the Taggerts. The place was certainly big enough.

Yes, she thought, settling back in the chair. It would work very nicely if she were to marry Mr. Montgomery.

The door burst open, and in rushed three of Terel's very best friends.

"There you are, Terel," Charlene said, ignoring Mary Alice. "We have been looking everywhere for you."

"Who is the divine man with Nellie?" Mae asked.

"With Nellie? Nellie's at home."

The girls looked at one another. They didn't often have news that Terel knew nothing of. They pulled the wooden chairs into a circle and gathered around Terel, noting, of course, that Mary Alice was listening with wide-open ears.

"He took Nellie to tea," Louisa said.

"And Nellie had on a disgusting old dress. The sleeves were much too small. Four years out of fashion if it's a day."

"And there was flour on her skirt."

"Whom was she with?" Terel demanded.

"Tall, very tall, dark hair and eyes, handsome—"

"Very handsome."

"Broad-shouldered and—"

"What was his *name?"* Terel asked, already getting angry because she knew who he was.

"Montgomery. Nellie said he's going to work for your father."

"No one who works for *my* father looks like *that,"* Louisa said, putting her hand to her breast.

Terel stiffened. "He does work for my father, and Nellie was merely showing him about Chandler. She—"

"Is that what she was doing when they were embracing on top of the wall by the park?"

Mary Alice gasped, then leaned forward to hear better.

"I cannot believe—" Terel began.

"At least a dozen people saw them!" Mae said. "The whole town is talking about it. Mr. Montgomery lifted Nellie up to the wall and—"

"Lifted *Nellie?"* Mary Alice said.

"Yes. Anyway," said Charlene, "he lifted her to the

wall, then climbed up with her, and in front of everyone he . . . he . . ."

"Pulled her into his arms," Mae said dreamily.

"And he took the pins from her hair! There they were, embracing for all the town to see, and he unfastened her hair, and we heard that he almost *kissed* her. In front of everyone!"

They sat there, looking at Terel, waiting for a response from her.

"I do not believe you," Terel said.

"You can ask anyone," Louisa said. "And their being on the wall wasn't the only thing that happened. According to Johnny Bowen and Bob Jenkins, Mr. Montgomery nearly attacked them on the street. All they did was ask Nellie about you."

"Ask about me?" Terel whispered. Johnny and Bob were two of her favorite suitors. They were adoring puppies, requiring nothing from Terel but always ready to do her bidding.

"Johnny said that Mr. Montgomery said that Nellie was not your social secretary." Mae turned to Louisa. "That's right, isn't it? That's what he said, isn't it?"

"Yes," Louisa answered. "Mr. Montgomery said Nellie wasn't going to answer questions about you, and Johnny said that Mr. Montgomery seemed quite taken with Nellie."

"In the tea shop," Mae said, "he looked at her as if he were—well—in love with her."

"With *Nellie?*" Mary Alice said. "With Nellie Grayson?"

Terel had heard more than she wanted to hear. She stood. "Mr. Montgomery is a very kind man, and he has a great deal of sympathy for women like Nellie. My poor sister has very little social life, and he felt pity for her, so he took her out for a day."

"I wish Mr. Montgomery would take pity on *me*," Mae said, but she quieted when Terel gave her a quelling look.

Terel jerked at her plum-dyed kid gloves. "I apologize if Mr. Montgomery's actions were misconstrued, and I would appreciate it if you would stop spreading gossip that has no basis in truth."

She pushed through the young women, purposely stepping on the lace of Mae's dress as she passed.

"What about your heart palpitations?" Mary Alice called after her.

"Her heart is fine, it's her temper that needs doctoring," Charlene said, and all four women dissolved into giggles.

Terel was very angry as she started walking home. How dare Nellie do this to her! As if she didn't have enough problems, what with so many other unmarried women in Chandler, to have her own sister betray her like this was more than she could bear!

She stormed all the way down Coal Avenue, and every block someone stopped her to ask about Nellie.

"Who was the heavenly man with her?"

"It looks like Nellie may beat you to the altar," Mr. Mankin said, laughing.

"I hear they're going to the Harvest Ball together,"

Mrs. Applegate said. "Do you think you'll be invited after what happened last year?"

"I never realized how pretty Nellie was until today," Leora Vaughn said. "I think I'll invite her to my garden party."

"Terel," Sarah Oakley said, "you must bring Nellie with you to next week's church social." She laughed. "This town isn't going to let you hide Nellie away any longer."

By the time Terel reached the sanctity of her house, her blood was boiling. She was ready to tear Nellie to pieces. How dare she act like this? How dare she call attention to herself like this?

Terel went first to the kitchen, then to the garden, but Nellie wasn't in either. Nor was she anywhere else in the house. It took Terel a few minutes to realize that Nellie was still out with Mr. Montgomery.

She sat down hard on a footstool in the parlor. Nellie was *always* home. Since Terel was a little girl, Nellie had been at home waiting for her. She remembered coming home from school, and Nellie would be in the kitchen ironing. Nellie had only been fourteen then, so she'd had to stand on a box to be high enough for the ironing board, but when Terel returned she'd get down and get milk and cookies for her.

Now Terel put her little handbag on the table and noted with disgust that the surface was dusty. Slowly, she got up and went back to the kitchen. Usually the place was neat and clean, but now the big table was covered with flour and there was a lump of dried, cracked dough to one side. The door had been left open, and flies buzzed over everything. The fire in the stove had gone out.

In the other rooms downstairs everything was dusty. If Nellie didn't constantly stay on that lazy Anna, the girl did nothing. Now, with Nellie having been gone most of the day, Anna was probably sleeping somewhere.

Upstairs, the rooms were as bad. The bathroom hadn't been cleaned, and her father's whisker-filled lather had dried on the basin. In Terel's room clothes were everywhere. This morning she'd had a difficult time deciding what to wear today, and all the clothes she'd decided against were still strewn about the room. On the bed was the pink taffeta that Terel had expressly asked Nellie to repair, but the skirt was still torn at the waist.

She went to her father's room, and it didn't look much better than her own. His clothes from the day before were on the floor, and six pairs of shoes had been set out for Nellie to polish, but all six were still dusty.

Terel moved down the hall. Nellie's room was, as always, neat and tidy, but it was the only bit of order in the chaotic house.

Thoughtfully, Terel went back downstairs to the parlor. From what the townspeople had been saying, whatever was going on between Nellie and Mr. Montgomery was serious. Serious as in permanent. Serious as in taking Nellie away.

Terel looked at the dusty parlor and thought about the rooms upstairs. If Nellie got married and left the house, who would have to see to the cooking and cleaning? She knew her father wouldn't bother himself. Although Nellie tended to look at their father through rose-colored glasses, Terel saw him for what he was. He was as tightfisted a man as had ever lived. Terel had an idea that her father's freight company made quite a bit of money, but Charles Grayson wasn't about to part with any more of it than he could help. That's why they lived in a very ordinary house and had only one very bad, but cheap, servant. Charles wouldn't part with his precious money to raise their standard of living.

Terel had learned how to deal with him. When she wanted new clothes she went to a store and charged them. Her father's pride kept him from refusing to pay the bills.

But Nellie knew nothing about their father. All Charles had to do was say he couldn't afford more servants and Nellie doubled her efforts to help make ends meet.

So what would happen if Nellie left, Terel thought. What if she went away and left Terel and Charles alone? Terel knew that Charles would make her life hell. He'd no doubt expect Terel to spend her days cooking and trying to get the lazy Anna to do something. If Terel did get out of doing the work, it would only be through waging enough battles to equal a war. Her father could be pleasant; cold, perhaps, but all right if his basic needs were taken care of and he didn't have to spend too much money. But he could be a tyrant over simple matters such as his dinner being late. Terel couldn't imagine what his temper would be like if she had to prepare his dinner. She didn't know the first thing about cooking.

"Nellie cannot leave before I do," Terel whispered. Under no circumstances was she going to allow Nellie to marry and leave Terel alone to take care of their father. Terel's jaw clamped shut. If nothing else, Nellie couldn't marry someone like Mr. Montgomery. Today was just an example of what would be said if fat, boring Nellie caught a man like that. She could hear Charlene now. "Your husband is nice, but he's not as rich or as handsome as Nellie's husband. Who would have thought that Nellie would get the catch of the season, all while wearing such ugly dresses? Terel, maybe you should have learned to cook."

No, Terel thought, she couldn't bear the ridicule— and she intended to see that there was no reason for her to bear it.

At six o'clock her father walked through the door, just as Terel knew he would, and she smiled, because Nellie still hadn't returned. She pulled out her hand-kerchief, sniffed a few times, and went running to her father.

"Oh, Papa," Terel wailed, throwing her arms about his neck, "I'm so glad you're home. I'm so very, very frightened."

With distaste, Charles pulled Terel's arms from

around his neck. He did not believe in physical displays of affection. "What has frightened you?"

Terel put her handkerchief to her face. "Nellie isn't home."

"Nellie isn't home?" Charles asked in the same tone he might use to say, The earth stopped turning? "Where is she?"

"I'm afraid to tell you. Oh, Papa, I hope our good name can overcome the scandal."

"Scandal? What is this?" He half pushed Terel into the dusty parlor. "Now tell me everything. Hold nothing back."

Terel, while giving a good show of weeping, told him all she knew and then some. "They were embracing on top of the wall! And everyone in town saw them. I wouldn't be surprised if people canceled their contracts with you after this. Nellie cares nothing about us, only about herself. There is no dinner prepared, and upstairs is a mess."

Charles's eyes widened, then he left the room to go upstairs. It was some minutes before he came down again. In spite of Terel's theatrics, Charles understood the problem very well. He wasn't concerned about Nellie's scandalous behavior causing him a loss of business, for if that were possible, Terel's behavior would have hurt his company years ago.

It was the unpolished shoes that caused him concern. Two years ago when Nellie had wanted to marry he had persuaded her not to. He'd known what his life would be like without Nellie. If Nellie left, he'd be alone to deal with Terel's laziness, with her refusal to do anything that didn't directly benefit herself.

When Charles had first met Jace Montgomery he'd known who he was. A year before someone had pointed him out as the son of the owner of Warbrooke Shipping. Charles had tried to get an introduction to him, but the man had left town before they could meet. A year later Charles had blessed his luck that, out of the blue, the man appeared and saved him from ruffians.

Immediately Charles had started planning. What a catch he'd be for a son-in-law! Jace would connect the Grayson family with Warbrooke Shipping. Charles imagined a vast land and sea company named Grayson-Warbrooke. So Charles had started talking about his beautiful daughter and had, after hours of talk, persuaded Jace to come to dinner.

Then everything had gone awry. Terel, as usual, hadn't listened when Charles had told her how important Montgomery was, and so she'd turned the man over to Nellie. Heaven only knew why he was interested in Nellie, but he had been from the first.

He can have Terel, Charles thought, but not Nellie. Or at least he couldn't have her until Terel was married and gone. Charles wasn't going to be left alone with his spoiled younger daughter.

"Fool man!" Charles muttered. What in the world did he see in Nellie? Nellie was to Terel as an old plow horse to a sleek racing filly.

He stepped back into the parlor. "I will send men

out to look for her," he said to Terel. "I do not believe our family can stand this scandal. I will forbid her to see Montgomery again." He gave Terel a piercing gaze. "Perhaps you could see that the man is introduced to Chandler society."

"I will do my best," Terel said solemnly. "You know, Papa, that I am always willing to help you."

Chapter Five

Nellie had been eating for three days. She couldn't seem to stop. She baked three pies and ate one of them. At the bakery she'd order four cakes and eat a whole one herself. She baked six dozen cookies and ate two dozen before they'd cooled. Every time she remembered the evening of the day she'd spent with Mr. Montgomery, she became ravenous.

The horror of that night—Terel crying, her father's disappointment in her—had haunted her every minute of every day since then. For three days now she'd lived in fear of people canceling their freight contracts because of Nellie's scandalous behavior. Her father had painted a bleak picture of the three of them being cast into the street with no food, having to survive a

Colorado winter in the open because Nellie was too selfish to care about anyone but herself.

That Nellie's behavior had been outrageous was verified by the many invitations that began arriving in her name.

"They believe you to be a woman of loose morals," Charles had said, throwing the invitations into the fire.

Part of Nellie wanted to point out that Terel received invitations yet wasn't considered a lewd woman. As though reading her thoughts, Terel had said that *she* hadn't been seen by the entire town embracing a man. *She* hadn't spent most of a night alone with a man in a park.

Nellie had tried to defend herself by pointing out that she'd been home by eight-thirty, but she'd burst into tears when her father asked if there was a chance she would bear the man's bastard.

Terel had talked to Nellie about how a worldly man like Mr. Montgomery only wanted Nellie because she was so innocent and he could get anything he wanted from her. "Look at yourself, Nellie. Why else would he want you?" Terel had said. "Men like him take advantage of women like you, women who will stay out all night with them, and then they marry respectable women. If he had any respect for you, he wouldn't have come to the back of the house and asked you to sneak away with him. A man who respects a woman treats her with respect."

Neither her father nor Terel let up on Nellie. They

talked and talked and talked. And Nellie ate and ate and ate.

She was sure they were right. She knew she had caused them great embarrassment, but sometimes, often late at night, she remembered the way Mr. Montgomery had looked at her. Nobody knew that he'd put his head in her lap, and Nellie was sure that if they did, they wouldn't hold out any hope that she could be saved; but sometimes she remembered the feel of his hair on her fingertips. She remembered how he'd asked her about what she liked to do in life. She remembered the tears on his cheeks when he'd sung the hymn.

In all her memories she could think of nothing that made him seem like the devious seducer that Terel seemed to think he was. Her father said that he flirted with all the pretty women who chanced to come into the freight office. And Terel said that in church on Sunday Mr. Montgomery sat between Mae and Louisa. Charles had said it was better for Nellie not to go to church that day, that she shouldn't be seen in public yet. He hoped her absence would help the gossip of her scandalous behavior die down. So on Sunday Nellie had remained home, and after Terel told her about Jace sitting with the other pretty, thin, younger women she'd eaten half a dozen cupcakes.

Now she was alone in the house, her father at his office, Terel at her dressmakers, and Anna sent off to the market. She was scouring pans from the previous night's dinner.

"Hello."

She turned to see him standing there, and the memories of that wonderful afternoon and evening together came back. She smiled at him before she remembered the last three days, then she frowned.

"You have to leave," she said, and she turned back to the dishes.

Jace put his bouquet of flowers on the table, went to her, took her shoulders, and turned her around. "Nellie, what's wrong? I haven't seen you in days. I've been by every evening, but your father said you were indisposed. You aren't ill, are you?"

No one had told her he'd come by. She moved away from him. "I am perfectly all right, and you have to leave. You cannot be alone with me. It isn't proper."

"Proper?" he asked, puzzled. If she hadn't been ill, then maybe she hadn't seen him because she didn't want to. "Nellie, have I done something to offend you?" He straightened. "Maybe at choir practice I . . ." He trailed off.

She gave him a startled look. Did he think his tears had offended her? "Oh, no, no, it's nothing like that. It's . . ." She couldn't tell him.

"What? What have I done wrong that you won't see me?"

To Nellie's disbelief, she burst into tears. She hid her face in her hands, and her shoulders shook with her weeping. Within moments Jace was there, his arm around her, and he was handing her a glass of brandy. "Drink this," he ordered when she was seated.

"I can't. I don't—"

"Drink it!"

She obeyed him, choking on the liquid but getting all of it down.

"Now," he said, taking the empty glass and sitting in front of her, "tell me what's been going on."

"We behaved scandalously," she said, and with the brandy in her it didn't seem like such an awful thing they had done.

Jace didn't understand. Maybe their behavior had been a little outrageous, but no one in Chandler seemed to have minded. In fact, everywhere he went people were curious about Nellie. It seemed that no one in town had even noticed her before.

He took her hands in his. "Was it our being alone? We could go out with other people if that bothers you." It might help him keep his hands off her, too, he thought.

"The wall," she said, sniffing.

"The wall?" He smiled. "You're upset because I hugged you on the wall? You were about to fall."

"I . . . I . . ." She couldn't tell him more, couldn't tell him of the possibility of people canceling contracts or say to him that he wasn't respecting her. When he looked at her as he did now she couldn't think clearly.

The sound of a footstep outside the kitchen door made her eyes widen in horror. "It's Terel. You have to go." There was panic in her voice.

"I'll say hello."

"No, no, no. Leave. You must leave."

Jace didn't know what the urgency was, but he had

no intention of leaving. He slipped into the pantry just as Terel entered the kitchen. Leaning against the shelves, he had a clear view into the kitchen and could see Nellie and her sister fully. Up until now he'd had eyes only for Nellie, but now it struck him as odd that there was such a contrast between the two sisters. Terel was dressed in an expensive wool suit, her hair coiffed and cared-for, while Nellie was wearing a dress that seemed quite old.

"Y-you're back early," Nellie said, stammering.

"Yes." Terel yanked off her kid gloves. "I couldn't stay in town and listen to more of the scandal. No one can talk of anything but you and that man."

Nellie's eyes darted to the pantry. "I don't think we should discuss this now. Maybe we should go into the parlor."

"I do not want to go to the parlor." Terel unpinned her hat. "I am famished. I couldn't even have luncheon because all anyone wanted to speak to me about was you and how you'd behaved with that man. I really couldn't bear it."

"Terel, please, let's go to the parlor. We can—"

"Look at the flowers! Nellie, why didn't you tell me I had flowers? Who are they from? Johnny? Bob? Not Lawrence, possibly?" Terel picked up the bouquet and searched for the card, then opened it. "It says," she read, "'to the most beautiful woman in the world.' How lovely. It *must* be Lawrence." She closed the card and then saw that it said "To Nellie, with love from Jace."

Terel had to read the card three times before she

really understood. She flung the flowers to the floor. "He has been here, hasn't he?" she cried. "He has been in this room. After all Father and I said to you, you continue with your licentious behavior. How could you, Nellie? How could you?"

"Terel, please," Nellie pleaded. "Couldn't we—"

"And brandy, too," she said, holding up the empty glass. "This has gone too far. Wait until I tell Father. Nellie, I never knew you were stupid. Don't you know that the people who love you know what's best for you? Don't you understand what he wants from a woman like you? He wants to get you drunk and—"

Terel's back was to the pantry, but Nellie was facing it, and to her horror Jace stepped into the kitchen, ready to do battle with Terel. Nellie shook her head violently, then sprinted across the kitchen. Terel fumbled with her handkerchief while Nellie pushed Jace back into the pantry. Her body was in the kitchen, but her outstretched arm was hidden inside the pantry.

"—and have his way with you," Terel finished.

At that Jace snorted.

"Are you laughing at me?" Terel asked in horror.

"No, of course not. I would never laugh at you. I—" Nellie couldn't say any more because Jace had taken her hand from his chest and begun nibbling at her fingertips.

"You don't know men like him, Nellie," Terel was saying. "He is a . . . well, he's a seducer of women."

Jace was biting the inside of her wrist, and she could feel the tip of his tongue on her skin.

"Nellie! Are you listening to me?"

"Yes," she said dreamily.

"You cannot trust men like him, and Father was right when he forbade you to see him again."

Jace paused in kissing Nellie's hand for just a second when Terel said that, but he continued. Besides kissing Nellie, he wanted to hear what the lying bitch had to say.

"Father told you about his flirting, and I myself saw him at church. He merely wants as many women as he can get. I don't know why he chose you as one of his . . . his conquests, but he has. Nellie, don't you know that we care about you and want what's best for you?"

Nellie could barely nod. Her sleeve had been pushed up to wash dishes, and now he was kissing the inside of her elbow.

"All the man wants from you is entry into Grayson Freight. He wants to be Father's partner. He would have tried to seduce me, but he knew I know too much about men to fall for his scandalous ways. *I* would never have let him humiliate me in public as he did you. So, knowing he couldn't get me, he went after you, and Nellie, you believed every word he said to you. Tell me, did he tell you you were beautiful?"

Nellie looked into the pantry at Jace. He looked up from her arm and nodded. "Yes," Nellie whispered. "He told me I was beautiful."

"There, you see. That proves he's a liar."

At that Jace dropped Nellie's arm and started out of the pantry, but Nellie put her hand on his chest and gave him a pleading look while Terel turned around to get a glass out of a cabinet.

"Terel, why don't you go upstairs and lie down? I'll bring your luncheon on a tray."

"Yes, perhaps that would be better. It has been a very trying day. You can't imagine the gossip I've had to listen to about my own sister."

Nellie started to pull away from Jace, but he wouldn't let her, so she stood where she was and gave Terel a weak smile. Sighing, Terel left the room.

Immediately, Nellie turned to him. "Mr. Montgomery, you cannot—" she began, but she couldn't say more because he pulled her into the pantry and into his arms.

He kissed her. At first Nellie was so shocked that she just stood there, her eyes open, his strong arms around her as he pulled her close to him.

"Nellie," he whispered as he moved to kiss her neck, "don't you understand that I'm not interested in your father's company? It's *you* I'm interested in."

She barely heard him as his lips moved down her neck. His big hands were on her body, and Nellie could feel her knees growing weak. He moved back to her mouth, kissing her gently at first; then, as Nellie relaxed against him, his kiss deepened. The tip of his tongue touched hers. At first she started to draw away from him, but he held her close.

It was some minutes before Nellie began to truly react to his touching her. She had no idea how much longing and desire were pent up inside her. She was a loving woman who had had no outlet for her love. Her hands moved from her sides to encircle him and pull him closer, and her breath came harder and faster as he continued kissing her.

"Nellie," he whispered, and he began to run his teeth and lips across her neck. She moved her arms up to bury her hands in his hair. She kissed his cheeks, his neck, running the tip of her tongue along his skin and feeling the whiskers. He smelled good; he felt good; he tasted good.

Within minutes Nellie could no longer see or think. She was all feeling, a great, huge, red mass of feeling.

"Nellie," Jace said, trying to pull away from her but finding it very difficult, "we have to stop." He lifted his head to look at her. Her face was flushed pink, her eyes closed, long, thick lashes against her soft cheek, and her lips were soft and full and parted invitingly.

"Nellie," he said again, and this time the sound was a groan. "I can't bear any more. We have to stop." He kissed her once gently, then pulled away. "I think your family might be a little shocked if they found us making love on the floor of the pantry."

Slowly Nellie opened her eyes and looked up at him. They were intimately pressed together, his leg between hers, and she remembered how wantonly she'd just behaved. "I . . . I'm sorry, Mr. Montgomery," she mumbled, releasing him. "I didn't mean . . ." She didn't know what to say.

"Quite all right," he said, smiling as though nothing had happened, but there was a glow of sweat on his brow.

Nellie was quite suddenly very embarrassed, and she started backing out of the pantry, her face red.

"Nellie." He caught her arm and pulled her close to him, but she pushed at him and gained her freedom.

"Mr. Montgomery, I am truly apologetic for . . . for my conduct," she muttered, moving into the kitchen. It was better not to look at him. If she didn't look at him again, perhaps she might forget how she had just behaved.

"Please look at me," he said, and when she wouldn't he took her by the shoulders and put his face close to hers. "You aren't going to believe what your sister said about me, are you? I haven't looked at any other woman in town except you. Those two over-dressed fillies in church sat by *me,* I didn't sit by them. And at your father's office I've never been anything but polite to the ladies."

She pulled away from him. "Mr. Montgomery, I have no idea what gave you the idea that your social life is my concern. You are free to pursue any and all of the pretty young women in town." She began slicing bread and beef to make a plate of food for Terel.

He could see that she didn't believe him. Damn that little brat Terel, he thought. Nellie believed everything she said. "I've never made any advances toward your sister, nor have I—"

"Are you implying that my sister was telling a falsehood?"

"If the shoe fits, wear it," he said before he thought.

She glared at him. "You may leave now, Mr. Montgomery. And I do not believe you should return."

"Nellie, I apologize. I didn't mean to say that about your sister, even if it is true. I meant—" He didn't continue because Nellie was looking at him with a great deal of anger. "Nellie, please walk out with me. Just leave everything here and walk with me. Let me show you how much you mean to me."

"As you just did in the pantry? No, Mr. Montgomery, I think not. I know what I am. I am an old maid who happens to have a rich father. You need not bother wasting any more of your time on me now that I have seen through you."

The pleading look left Jace's face and was replaced with one of rage. "I have never been dishonest with you," he said through clenched teeth, "and I do not like being accused of dishonesty." He stepped toward her, and Nellie stepped back. The anger on his face was frightening. "Someday, Nellie, you're going to have to make a choice—either your own life or your family's. I'm willing to help, but not when I'm called a liar and told I'm courting a woman merely to get her father's money. If you took a little time to get to know me, you'd find out I'm not like that. I'm—" He broke off. He wasn't about to tell her what he was like. If she believed her sister, believed what someone else told her instead of what she knew to be true, that was her problem. He wasn't going to defend himself to her.

He took his hat from the table. "If you want to be an

old maid, that's your decision. It was nice meeting you, Nellie," he said, and then he turned on his heel and left the kitchen.

For a moment Nellie was too stunned to think. She stared at the empty doorway, unable to move.

So, she thought at last, Terel had been right. He wanted only her father's money. When he knew he wasn't going to get it, when he knew Nellie had been told of his devious plan, he left.

For a moment Nellie considered going after him. For a second it occurred to her that it didn't matter whether he wanted her for her father's money or not. Whatever had caused his interest in her, the afternoon and evening they had spent together had been the happiest hours of her life. She closed her eyes and remembered being on the wall with him, the way he'd made her feel light and pretty. She remembered his head being in her lap as they talked. She thought of the way he'd sung the hymn and how the tears had coursed down his cheeks. And today in the pantry. She had never before felt passion, and it was a new and heady experience. She folded her arms across her chest and rubbed her forearms.

Money, she thought. All he'd wanted was her father's money, and as Terel said, he was courting a fat old maid to get it.

Behind her the kitchen door swung open. "She wants her lunch," Anna said, sullen at having to do some work.

Nellie came back to the present. "Yes, I'm coming," she said, gathering up the tray and food.

Terel was sitting on the bed reading, pillows propped behind her, her silk skirt wrinkled beneath her. Nellie put the tray across her lap and began hanging up Terel's clothes.

"There is no flower."

"What?" Nellie asked absently. She kept seeing Jace's eyes. He had been so angry at her. Maybe she shouldn't have accused him as she had. Perhaps she should have gathered a little more proof that his intentions were dishonorable. Maybe—

"You always put a flower on my tray," Terel said, as though she were on the verge of tears. "Oh, Nellie, you don't care about us anymore, only about him."

Nellie took the tray off Terel's lap, pulled her young sister into her arms and stroked her hair. My child, Nellie thought. Terel is the only child I'll ever have. For a moment she felt like crying, too. Perhaps the only chance she'd ever have of having her own home and family had just walked out.

"I do care about you," Nellie said. "I've been so busy lately that I just forgot the flower. It doesn't mean I no longer care for you."

"You like Father and me better than *him?*"

"Of course I do."

Terel clasped Nellie to her. "You wouldn't run off with him and leave us, would you?"

Nellie pulled away and smiled at Terel. "A fat old maid like me? Who would have me?"

Terel sniffed. *"We* want you. Father and I want you."

Nellie was beginning to feel hungry. She moved away from Terel and replaced the tray on her lap. "You should eat your lunch and perhaps take a nap. You're probably tired from all the worry."

"Yes, I guess I am, but Nellie, don't go."

Reluctantly Nellie sat on the edge of the bed. Hunger was gnawing her stomach.

"He really is gone?" Terel asked, her mouth full. "You don't have him lurking downstairs somewhere, do you?"

"No." Nellie was getting hungrier by the second.

"Oh, Nellie, you don't know what a curse it is to be young and beautiful as I am. Men have the most awful motives for wanting to be near you." She broke off a piece of bread Nellie had baked just that morning and gave her sister a hard look. "Have you been invited to the Harvest Ball?"

Nellie could feel her face flushing. "Yes," she whispered.

Terel set her luncheon tray on the table by the bed, then put her hands over her face. "I have not been invited. I am the only person in town who is not going."

Again, Nellie pulled her sister into her arms. "You may have my invitation. I don't guess I'll be going now, and besides, what would I wear to something like that?"

"I can't take your invitation. The Taggerts don't think I'm socially acceptable. Me! Everyone knows the Taggerts are little better than coal miners. Oh, Nellie, I wish . . ."

"You wish what?"

Terel pulled away, sniffing. "I wish I were the most popular girl in Chandler. I wish I were invited to every party, every outing there was. I wish no one in Chandler would consider giving a party without me there."

Nellie smiled. "Then that's what I wish, too."

"Do you really?"

"Yes, I really do. I wish you were the most popular girl Chandler has ever seen, and that you had more invitations than you could possibly accept."

"Yes, I'd like that," Terel said, smiling.

"That would make you happy?"

"Oh yes, Nellie, I would be very happy if I were popular. That's all I'd ever ask out of life."

"Then I very much hope that you get your wish," Nellie said. "Now, why don't you take a nap? I have some work to do."

"Yes," Terel said, smiling and stretching out on the bed. She was wrinkling her dress, but it didn't matter to her; she didn't have to iron it.

Nellie quietly took the tray and left the room. In the kitchen, when she was alone again, she thought more about Jace. If he wasn't after her for her father's money, then she had insulted him greatly. What had he said about courting? Something about having the woman he was courting call him a liar.

The more she thought, the hungrier Nellie became. She tried to control her appetite by sheer force of will, but with every thought she had her hunger increased. Jace had said she had choices, that she was choosing her family over herself. Of course she was choosing her family over herself! Wasn't that what a person was supposed to do? Didn't the Bible teach that a person had to give to receive?

Nellie slammed bread dough on the table. What a selfish man Mr. Montgomery must be to not realize that life's greatest joy was in giving to others. Look at how she and her family gave to one another. Her father gave his love and support to his two daughters, and Terel also gave love. In return for their love Nellie cooked for them, kept the house clean, waited on them, ran errands, listened to them, cared about them, and—

To stop the flow of thoughts, Nellie began to eat. She ate anything she could find: five slices of beef, half a pie, a jar of peaches, the heel of a loaf of bread; and when the kitchen was denuded of food, she moved to the pantry. When she entered the pantry she remembered Jace, remembered the way he'd held her, the way he'd kissed her.

"I don't care if he wants me only for my father's money," she whispered, and then, to keep from crying, she opened a jar of strawberry jam and began eating it with her fingers.

It was while Nellie was in the pantry that Terel's first invitation arrived, and by the time she awoke from her nap five invitations were waiting for her.

"How?" Terel whispered when Nellie handed them to her.

"Wishes," Nellie said, smiling, glad to see Terel so happy. "You wished for it, and you got it."

Terel clasped the invitations to her breast for a moment, then opened her eyes wide. "What am I going to *wear?* Oh, Nellie, you'll have to get my dressmaker and tell her to bring fabric samples and patterns."

"I can't go, I have to prepare dinner. I'll send Anna, or maybe you should go to her."

"I can't. One of the invitations is for tea today. And you can't send Anna. She'll never get the message right. You'll have to go yourself, Nellie. If only Father would put in a telephone!"

"Terel, I haven't time to——"

Terel turned on her. "I thought you wished for me to be popular. I thought you really, truly wanted me to be popular."

"I do, but . . ."

Terel put her arm around Nellie. "Please help me. If I meet a lot of people, perhaps I'll find a man to marry, and then I'll be out of your hair forever. Maybe this time next year I won't be living here, and you won't have to bother with my needs. Then you can have all the free time you want with just Father to care for."

Nellie didn't like to think of living alone with her father. The prospect of a house without Terel was too gloomy to contemplate. "I'll go," Nellie said. "You get dressed."

It was hours later that Nellie was again in the

kitchen. Her father would be home soon, and dinner wasn't ready. She had managed to get the dressmaker to Terel and had helped Terel dress and do her hair before Howard Bailey came for her in his carriage. Now she was hurriedly trying to get the evening meal ready.

"What is going on?" Charles Grayson asked, bursting into the kitchen. "Anna said Terel has spent a fortune on dresses today."

Nellie made a silent vow to have words with Anna. "Terel began receiving invitations this afternoon, and she felt she needed new clothes for the occasions."

"Terel *always* believes she needs new clothes." He looked at the table, noting the vegetables that had been chopped but not cooked. "Is Terel the reason dinner is going to be late?"

"I was helping her, yes."

"You were playing with Terel and neglecting your work?"

Nellie gripped the rolling pin so hard her knuckles turned white. "I will have dinner on the table at six."

"Good," Charles said, then he seemed to search for something else to say. "Anna said you wished for Terel to receive the invitations."

"It was a bit of nonsense, that's all."

"Well, if you're having wishes come true, then wish that I get the money to pay for all these new dresses." He turned away and left the kitchen.

For a moment, Nellie closed her eyes. "I wish Father would be very successful," she whispered. "I hope he makes more than enough to pay for Terel's dresses."

She opened her eyes, then smiled. Such nonsense, she thought. Wishes don't come true, because if they did . . . She thought of Jace but then pushed the image from her mind. Father, she thought. I hope he gets what he wants.

Chapter Six

Kane Taggert stood at the window of his office and watched his cousin pacing through the garden. When his wife came to stand behind him Kane didn't turn.

"How long has he been there?" Houston asked.

"This is the third day. He goes off to work for that Grayson man, but he spends the rest of the day wanderin' around out there." Kane frowned. "He's beginnin' to annoy me."

"I would imagine his pain is a great deal worse than yours," Houston said.

He turned to look at her. "I wouldn't go through that courtin' time again for all the money in the world."

She smiled and kissed his cheek, but as she started

to move away he pulled her to him. "Think ol' Jace is in hell?" he asked.

"I would guess so," she answered sadly. "No one in Chandler has seen Nellie and him together for days, but Terel is everywhere."

Kane kissed his wife, then released her and went back to his desk. "Nellie Grayson." There was wonder in his voice. "How come he wants a woman who's so—"

"Don't say it," Houston said quickly. "Nellie is a lovely woman. Whenever that family of hers allows her out, she does a great deal of church work. Her heart is loving and kind, and I think Jace sees that in her."

"Yeah, maybe she's a great person, but Jace ain't a bad-lookin' guy, so how come he wants a woman who's so"—he looked at his wife—"so big?"

"Jocelyn's mother is LaReina."

Kane obviously had no idea who that was.

"We heard her sing in Dallas."

"Oh," he said, disappointed. "An opera singer. What's that got to do with Jace likin' Nellie?"

"By tradition, opera singers are Rubenesque, and from what Jace has told us, he grew up surrounded by his mother's friends."

Kane had some trouble understanding what his wife was saying, but then he smiled. "Oh, I see. You mean Jace has always been around fat ladies."

Houston's eyes narrowed. "Any woman with a voice so blessed as to be a coloratura soprano does *not* deserve to be dismissed as a 'fat lady.'"

Kane continued smiling. "To each his own, I guess. But f . . ." He stopped. "Plump or not, it looks like Jace ain't exactly havin' an easy path down the road to gettin' the woman he wants. You better go talk to him."

Houston watched her cousin by marriage disappear down a path. "I was thinking the same thing."

Kane gave a snort of laughter. "Now things'll get straightened out."

Houston didn't answer as she went outside into the garden.

"Hello, Jocelyn," she said softly, and then she smiled at him when he turned toward her. There were dark circles under his eyes, and he looked as though he hadn't shaved this morning. In the right clothes, she thought, he'd look like a pirate.

"How's Nellie?" she asked.

Jace jammed his hands in his trouser pockets and turned away. "I don't know. She won't see me."

"Did you quarrel?"

"Yes. I think so." He gave a sigh, then sat down heavily on a stone bench. "Houston, that is the *strangest* family I have ever seen."

She sat down beside him and waited for him to continue.

Jace leaned back against a tree and stretched out his long legs. "When I met Charles Grayson, all he could talk about was his beautiful daughter. From the way he talked I got the impression he knew about my family's money and wanted to marry off some ugly daughter to me. I don't know why, maybe I was intrigued, but I went to his house to meet this daughter. I went an hour early, when I knew Charles wouldn't be home."

Jace closed his eyes for a moment. "Nellie was everything her father said she was. She is beautiful, kind, and I could see in her eyes that there was so much inside her. From that first night I wanted to take her away with me and show her the world."

"But her family stopped you," Houston said.

Jace's face showed his puzzlement. "I don't understand them. It seems that I can have the younger sister if I want her, but not Nellie."

He stood, and his face grew angry. "Three days ago I went to see Nellie, and she was afraid of her family seeing me. I had to hide in the pantry like the grocery boy who isn't supposed to be there. That . . . that sister of hers came in and told Nellie one lie after another about me, saying I was after her father's money—as if the man had any."

Houston suppressed a smile over the vanity of rich men. "What do you plan to do now?"

Jace let his hands drop to his sides; his shoulders slumped. "I don't know. Nellie won't see me. I've sent flowers, two letters, I even sent her a puppy, but everything was returned to me with no explanation, nothing." He looked at Houston. "Is there a Western way of courting that I don't know about? The last time I courted a woman I sent her flowers, we walked out together, one day I asked her to marry me, and she said yes. I don't remember courtship being so difficult."

Houston patted the seat by her, and Jace sat down again. "Since I talked to you about the Harvest Ball I've talked to some people about Nellie. Tell me, is Charles Grayson an ungenerous man?"

Jace rolled his eyes. "He could give Scrooge lessons. He pays his employees as little as possible and docks their wages for every minute they're late. I can hardly bear to stay in the office. Three days ago he got a contract out of Denver—I don't know how, since he expects to make vast profits on every deal—but he did, and he fired two freight drivers because he said the other drivers could work longer hours. He's a mean, miserly man, and if it weren't for Nellie I wouldn't have anything to do with him."

"That explains why he expects Nellie to do the work of a household full of servants. He works Nellie harder than his employees, and he pays her even less than he does them."

Jace was quiet for a moment. "Grayson wouldn't want to lose an employee who worked hard and took none of his money."

"Exactly."

Jace leaned his head back against a tree. "I guess I've been so enraptured with Nellie that I never really looked at her family. That younger daughter is a real bitch. Oh, sorry."

"Quite all right, since I happen to agree, but she's quite pretty, and lately quite popular. For the last few days she's been in great demand at every social function."

"She's not half as pretty as Nellie," Jace said,

smiling. "Nellie has a way of looking at a man . . . well, she makes me feel as though I could do anything. Since I met her I've been doing some sketches for a steering mechanism for a boat. It's the first time I've drawn anything since . . ." He trailed off, remembering Julie's death, but for once not feeling empty.

"They've poisoned her mind against me," Jace said softly. "They tell her I'm up to no good, then tell her she can't see me. I don't even get an opportunity to defend myself. If I could just get her away from them for a while, maybe I could show her that I'm not a bad sort."

"You can't kidnap her," Houston said thoughtfully. "Women don't take well to kidnapping."

Jace didn't smile. "I've already dismissed the idea. I thought of kidnapping her onto a boat and sailing her around the world, but Colorado is too far from the ocean."

Houston blinked. "There must be some less drastic measure you could take. Is there something Nellie loves, loves above all else in the world?"

"Kids," he said quickly. "I think maybe that's why she does anything her bratty sister tells her to do. She thinks of Terel as her kid. I volunteered to give her a few kids of her own, but now I don't guess I'll get the chance."

Houston stood. "There. You have your answer."

Jace looked blank. "You mean impregnate her?"

She grimaced. "Of course not. Give Nellie what she really wants and she'll come to you."

"I don't understand."

"Think about it, Jocelyn," she said as she put her hand on his shoulder. "If you want Nellie, it looks as though you're going to have to fight for her. If you want her enough and fight hard enough, I think you can get her, but it's not going to be an easy courtship. One of those to a customer."

Jace took Houston's hand and kissed it. "You're not going to help me figure out what to do, are you?"

"No. You just have to open your eyes and look, and you'll be able to see what needs to be done."

He smiled at her. "I wish I'd met you before Kane did. I would have given him a run for his money."

She smiled. "He had me picked out since I was a child. I never had a chance, and neither would you. Now, I must go in and see to my children."

As she walked away Jace called out after her, "Would you like a puppy?"

"Send it over," she said, laughing.

When he was alone Jace thought about what Houston had said. There *must* be a way to win Nellie.

Nellie was in the kitchen, which had to be a hundred and ten degrees. The stove was going at full heat to cook the pastries for the tea Terel was giving the next day, and to warm the six irons on top. Nellie was bending over the heavy ironing table, applying a fluting iron to the delicate ripples in Terel's silk blouse.

The changes in the Grayson household in the past week had tripled Nellie's work. Terel's new popularity had greatly increased her need for freshly washed and ironed clothing. Nellie had tried to get Anna to help with the load, but the stupid girl had left a hot iron on the skirt of one of Terel's best dresses and ruined it. Afterward, Charles said Nellie had better see to the ironing herself as he could not afford to have clothes ruined.

So Nellie was trying to keep up with Terel's ever-increasing wardrobe and to cook for the many guests now flooding the house. Terel said she couldn't accept invitations without extending some herself.

Through all the ironing and the cleaning and the cooking, Nellie kept thinking of that glorious afternoon she had spent with Mr. Montgomery. She also thought of the day he'd come to the kitchen and kissed her in the pantry.

She slammed an iron down on a pink brocade skirt. So much for courting, she thought. She hadn't had a word from him since that day in the pantry. Terel often told of him, though—of how he was at one social event after another and how he had been seen often in the company of Olivia Truman.

"Terel was right about him," she muttered, trying to make herself feel grateful to her sister for warning her away from the man. But every time she thought of the afternoon with him, a part of her wanted to see him again. Part of her didn't care if he was after her father's money or not.

"Hello."

Nellie jumped half a foot at the sound of the voice, and when she saw Jace, before she thought, she smiled warmly at him. Quickly, she caught herself. "You should not be here, Mr. Montgomery," she said sternly, trying to look away from him, but in truth she wanted to memorize his features.

"I know," he said, humbly, "and I apologize. I came to ask for your help."

"Help?" she asked. Remember, she told herself, this man is only interested in your father's money. He is the worst kind of scoundrel. "I'm sure you can find someone else to help you with whatever you need."

"I need a recipe."

She blinked at him. "A recipe?" For what, to make cakes for Miss Truman? She chided herself. What he did was none of her concern.

He took a little notebook and a stubby pencil from inside his jacket. "I've been told you're one of the best cooks in Chandler, so I thought maybe you'd know how to make biscuits. Mind if I sit down?"

"No, of course not." She put her iron down. "What do you want a biscuit recipe for?"

"I just need it. Now, let's see, you need flour, but how much?"

"How many biscuits do you want to make?" She walked to stand by the table.

"Enough for six kids, so how much flour?"

"Why can't their mother make biscuits?"

"She's sick. How many biscuits can I make with fifty pounds of flour? Do I need anything else? I just add water, right?"

"Flour and water makes glue, not biscuits." She sat down across from him.

"Oh, right, glue," he said, writing. "I need yeast, don't I?"

"Not for biscuits. Whose children are they?"

"One of the freighters who used to work for your father. Your father fired him, and the poor man has six kids to feed and a sick wife. I got their father a job hauling a load of corn to Denver, but there's nobody to take care of the kids, so I thought I'd go cook something for them. Now, about these biscuits—if you don't use yeast, what do you use?"

"Did you go to Reverend Thomas at the church? He always has people ready to help. One of the women—"

He gave her a sad look. "I thought of that, but I feel responsible for these people. Maybe if I hadn't taken the job with your father, the driver wouldn't have been fired. You see, I helped make out the job estimate that got the new contract for your father. So, about these biscuits—"

"Why did my father fire him?"

"The fewer people he has to pay, the more money he makes," Jace said simply. "Baking soda? Is that something that goes into biscuits? What about lard? You wouldn't know how to make flapjacks, would you? You use yeast in them?"

Nellie stood. "No, you don't use yeast in pancakes. Mr. Montgomery, I'm going with you."

"With me?"

"There seem to be six hungry children who need help, and I'm going with you to give them that help."

"I'm not sure you should."

"Why not?" she demanded.

"I'm afraid your father might not like it, and what about your reputation? Driving twenty miles out into the country alone with me, and you've heard what a womanizer I am."

"It seems that these children's hunger was caused by my father, therefore it is my Christian duty to help them." She looked down at him, at his dark hair and eyes, at his broad shoulders. "My reputation is nothing compared to hungry children. I must take my chances with you."

He leaned back in his chair and smiled to show the dimple in his cheek. "We all must make sacrifices at times."

Nellie put out of her mind that she was leaving a heap of Terel's dresses yet to be ironed. She pulled the pastries out of the oven, started to let them cool, then, on impulse, dumped them all into a canvas bag. Tomorrow there would be no home-baked goods for Terel's tea, and supper tonight was almost sure to be late.

She wrote a hurried note to her father telling him where she was going, then turned to Jace. "I'm ready."

He smiled at her again and distracted her so much that she didn't see him take the note she'd written and stick it in his pocket. "I have a wagonload of food outside so we can leave now." Before anyone sees us and stops us, he thought.

"With baking powder?"

"Sure," he said, having no idea what was in the wagon. He'd just told the grocer to fill it and never looked at the contents.

Jace got a great deal of pleasure helping Nellie onto the wagon, and once she was seated he flipped the reins of the horses and took off. He wanted to get out of Chandler as fast as possible. He held his breath until the houses were in the distance and open country surrounded them.

He reined in the horses and slowed them to a walk. "How have you been, Nellie?"

Nellie looked at him, so handsome, his strong white teeth showing against lips she knew to be soft and warm, and swallowed. Perhaps she had been hasty in her decision to leave with him. "All right," she mumbled, trying to move away from him on the seat, but the way he drove, with his legs wide apart, caused his thigh to press against hers.

"I hear you and your sister have been receiving invitations to everything in town."

"Terel has, not me."

He looked at her, surprised. "Yesterday Miss Emily asked me why you'd been refusing all the invitations sent to you. People are beginning to think you're snubbing them."

It was Nellie's turn to be surprised. "But I haven't been invited. All the invitations have been to Terel."

"Hmmm," he said, looking back at the horses.

"Mr. Montgomery, are you implying that my sister kept the invitations from me?"

"Did you get the flowers I sent? I've sent you flowers every day for the past week."

"I received no flowers," she said softly.

"How about the two letters I sent?"

Nellie didn't answer.

"The puppy?"

"Puppy?"

"Cute little collie pup. It was returned to the hotel with a note from you saying you didn't want anything from me, nor did you ever want to see me again. He was a frisky pup, wasn't he?"

"I never saw him," Nellie mumbled.

"I'm sorry, I couldn't hear you."

"I didn't see the puppy," Nellie said louder. Could Terel or her father have kept her from knowing of these gifts and messages? Why would they do that? Terel had said that no word had come from Mr. Montgomery. "How is Olivia Truman?"

"Who?"

"Olivia Truman. She's a very pretty redhead. Her father owns quite a bit of land outside Chandler."

"I don't remember meeting her."

"You must have met her at one of the social events you've attended this week. The garden party? The box lunch? The church supper?"

Jace was beginning to understand. "Since I saw you last I have worked in your father's office, bent over a stack of dirty ledgers, and I have spent my evenings at my cousin's house. Houston will tell you that I've had dinner at their house every night this week, and my social life has consisted of giving about a million piggy back rides to those three kids."

Nellie was silent for a while. Every evening Terel had told her where she had seen Mr. Montgomery and with whom he'd been. One of them was not telling the truth and instinctively she knew it was Terel. Perhaps she meant to protect me, Nellie thought. Perhaps she was doing what she thought was best for me.

"How are you enjoying Chandler, Mr. Montgomery?" she asked, trying to make polite conversation.

"I'm enjoying it quite a lot now that you're beside me again," he answered.

Nellie didn't know what to say in reply. Was he the villain portrayed by her father and Terel, or was he as he seemed to her? She'd never had any reason before to doubt her family, but now there were things puzzling her.

They were some miles out of town when, coming over a hill, Jace looked down into a valley and saw the freight driver's wagon, loaded with corn and still sitting beside the cabin. He knew without a doubt that the man hadn't understood his plan.

Jace brought the wagon to a halt. "Nellie, I have to leave you here. I'm afraid that the driver's wife may have some contagious illness. I couldn't bear to expose you to it."

"Don't be absurd," she was saying, even as he came around the wagon to help her down. "If you can be exposed to it, so can I." But he didn't listen to her, just put his strong arms up to help her down. "Mr. Montgomery, I want to go with you. I—"

He kissed her softly but distractedly. "I'll be back for you as fast as I can, honey. Don't worry."

He leaped onto the wagon, flicked the reins, and left in a cloud of dust.

Nellie stood back, coughing, and watched him. "Honey," she murmured. No one had ever called her honey before.

By the time Jace reached the Everetts' cabin he was in a fine temper. "I'll wring his neck," he muttered as he pulled the horses to a halt and leaped down from the wagon. The front door of the cabin was open to the Indian summer warmth, and inside the whole family—two adults and six kids—were quietly eating lunch. The table was loaded with ham and vegetables and corn bread, and a pie stood waiting on the sideboard.

"What the hell are you doing here?" Jace bellowed, causing all eyes to look at him. "I apologize for my language, ma'am," he said, removing his hat as he stepped inside, "but what are you doing here?"

"I was up all night loading corn," Frank Everett said. "I just got up."

Jace glared at him. "You haven't told her, have you?"

Frank leaned back in his chair. He wore his dirty longjohns with suspenders over them. He yawned and scratched his arm. "To tell you the truth, Mr. Montgomery, I ain't sure I understood it all."

Jace's anger left him and was replaced by embarrassment. He looked down at the toe of his shoe.

The man's wife stood. "Won't you sit and eat? We

got more'n enough. I guess you're the man that gave Frank the job haulin' the corn."

"Yes, I am." Now that he was here, what he'd planned to do seemed ridiculous. "But I can't eat. I have someone waiting for me."

Frank, looking puzzled, turned to his wife. "He wants you to be sick and he wants the kids to be hungry, then he wants to bring a young lady out here and save us all. Don't make no sense to me."

Mrs. Everett frowned for a moment as she thought, then her face lit with a smile. "Why, Frank, he's in love."

Jace's face turned even redder as the older children began to titter.

Mrs. Everett took over. "I'd be glad of a few days of rest, and if one of them town ladies wants to save us, she sure can." She looked at her children. "Sarah, I saw Lissie makin' eyes at that oldest Simons boy you're sweet on. And Frank Jr., your brother said he could outride and outshoot you any day of the week."

The oldest girls immediately went into an ear-splitting argument, and the two oldest boys, without a word spoken, fell on each other, fists flying. The youngest children, scared, started crying.

Frank looked at his family, at the girls just about to start pulling hair, and at his sons rolling about on the floor trying to kill each other, at the babies screaming so energetically that their mouths were bigger than their faces, then back at Jace. "You *sure* you wanta court a woman?" he yelled over the noise.

Mrs. Everett pushed past her husband. "Go on,"

she shouted to Jace. "You go get your young lady and bring her here. We'll be the neediest family she ever saw."

Jace nodded and went out into the relative peace of the cool Colorado air. He took his time driving back to Nellie. He didn't like staging this farce but he knew of no other way to get her out from under her family's thumb. She was sitting quietly waiting for him when he returned, and slowly they drove back to the cabin. By the time he got there he was ready to tell Nellie that he'd lied to her and that Mrs. Everett wasn't ill, and since Jace had given Mr. Everett a job, the family wasn't starving. But the minute they entered the cabin he was glad he'd done what he had. All six children, with tearstained cheeks, looked sad and forlorn. There wasn't a bite of food in the house; Mrs. Everett, looking very poorly, was lying in bed; and Frank and his wagon were gone.

Nellie took over at once. Within minutes she had the wagon unloaded, the stove going, and food cooking. From the beginning Jace had had an idea of what Nellie was really like, but his ideas were based on what he sensed, not what he'd seen. Now, out from under the influence of her dreadful family, she blossomed. Here there was no Terel telling her she was plain and fat and old. Her father wasn't there to remind her that she should be grateful for everything she had.

All that was in the cabin were eight people who thought she was wonderful, for Jace saw that if Nellie liked children, it was nothing to how much children liked Nellie. Within an hour of her arrival all six kids were talking to her at once. The smallest girl dragged out a doll for Nellie to repair, the boys were bragging of their exploits, and the oldest girls wanted to know all about the young men in town. Nellie told them that Jace was a relative of the very handsome seventeen-year-old Zachary Taggert, and after that there was no peace for Jace.

Nellie also took care of Mrs. Everett, bringing her a plate of food on a tray, fluffing her pillows, and in general, making her more comfortable than she'd ever been in her life.

Jace sat back in the bustle and watched and participated. He had never felt more at home in his life. He held a child on his lap and watched Nellie rolling out dough for a pie while she helped one of the boys with his sums. The oldest girls had gone to gather eggs and milk the cow while a boy fed the horses.

Jace looked across the head of the child in his lap and exchanged a smile with Nellie. This was all he'd ever wanted in his life. He had never been like his brother Miles, who wanted lots of women. No, Jace had just wanted a home with a wife and some kids, a place of safety and security, a place where he knew he'd be loved.

Nellie looked across the table at him, sitting there with that blond child on his lap, and she knew that he had never lied to her about anything. If he said he cared for her, then he did care for her. If he said he hadn't been out with other women, then he hadn't. She smiled at him, and it flashed through her mind that she'd like to keep smiling at him for the rest of her life.

By the time she'd cooked enough food to last for a few days, bathed the youngest two children, and gotten the rest of them in bed, it was nine o'clock at night and fully dark outside.

"I must get back to my family," Nellie said to Jace in the quiet stillness of the house. "But I hate to leave Mrs. Everett alone."

Jace took her hand and led her outside into the cool, clean air. Leaving the warmth of the house made her shiver. He pulled her back against his chest and wrapped his arms around her. "It'll be winter soon. Winter and snow and blazing fires and—"

"Christmas," she said.

"I know what I want for Christmas," he said, nuzzling her neck.

"Jace . . ."

"It's nice to know I've finally graduated from being Mr. Montgomery."

She leaned back against him. Here and now, standing so close to this man, she could almost believe that the moment could last forever. "I must go home," she said, but she made no effort to move out of his embrace.

"There are no lanterns for the wagon and no moon to speak of. We'll have to stay here tonight." He clasped her tighter. "I guess you'll be safe with all these chaperons."

She turned around in his arms. "I'm not sure I want to be safe."

She felt him draw in his breath, then he kissed her, long and deeply and lovingly, letting her know how he was coming to care for her more each day.

From the porch came a set of giggles.

"We have an audience," he whispered as he nibbled her ear.

"So it seems." She was reluctant to release him, but the giggles came again, so she dropped her arms and he took her hand in his and they started back toward the cabin. There was the sound of children scurrying into the cabin ahead of them.

"Our kids behave like that and I'll tan their backsides," Jace said.

Nellie laughed. "I can't imagine you striking anyone, least of all a child."

"Maybe not. Maybe I'll just put our bedroom on one end of the house and the kids' on the other."

It wasn't until later, when Nellie was snuggled down into bed with the girls, that she realized they had been talking as though their marriage was a foregone conclusion. She went to sleep smiling.

Chapter Seven

When Nellie awoke the next morning she was still smiling. There was a great deal to do in preparing breakfast for six kids and three adults, but she loved the bustle and activity. The children saw that Jace was a pushover when it came to discipline, and they talked their way out of doing their chores for the day. It was only when the unmilked cow was bawling, there was no wood for the stove, and no water had been brought from the well that Nellie went after them.

Jace teased her, untied her apron strings, then talked Nellie into playing with them. The boys piled bales of hay up to the barn roof, then made a slide. After much teasing and laughing, Jace and the kids persuaded Nellie to take a turn on the slide, too. Jace sat down behind her, his legs stretched out beside hers, and they went sliding down together, landing at the bottom in a heap of straw and petticoats. Jace tried to "help" her right herself and regain her dignity, but his hands seemed to be all over her at once, and she was laughing so helplessly that she fell back into the straw, the children tumbling on top of her and Jace.

When she came up for air she didn't at first recognize the sheriff standing over them.

"Hello," she managed to say, pulling straw from her hair and righting a child at the same time.

"Nellie," the sheriff said, "did you know that all of Chandler is looking for you? There are rumors that you've been kidnapped, or worse."

Nellie sat blinking at the man. "But I left a note," she managed to say, and she turned to look at Jace, half-buried in the straw beside her. He looked away, and she knew without a doubt that he'd stolen the note.

"You'd best come back with me, Nellie," the sheriff said, "and show everyone that you're all right."

"Nellie," Jace said, his hand on her shoulder, "I'll go back with you. I'll explain that it was my fault that you were missing."

"You'd better not," she whispered. She knew what waited for her at home: her father's anger, Terel's tears, and her own feelings of guilt for having worried them so. "I must face them alone, and besides, you need to stay with the children until Mrs. Everett is well."

Jace walked her to the sheriff's buggy, and as she

started to mount the steps he turned her toward him. "Nellie, don't let them be too hard on you. I'll see your father later today and explain."

"No," she said quickly, "you might lose your job."

He smiled at her. "Don't worry about my job." In front of everyone, he took her in his arms and kissed her. "I have to go to Denver tomorrow on business, but I'll be back the day of the Harvest Ball. I'll see you then." He kissed her again. "Save every dance for me."

She nodded at him and reluctantly released him, and he helped her into the buggy.

"Take good care of my girl, sheriff," Jace called as the buggy started to move.

Nellie looked out the back and waved at Jace and the children and Mrs. Everett standing on the porch in her nightgown. She brushed away a tear and turned to look at the road ahead.

What greeted her at home was worse than she had imagined. She had never seen her father in such a rage.

"You could have been killed for all I knew," he yelled. "Your sister and I, not to mention half the town, have been up all night looking for you. We have been worried sick about you while you . . . you . . ." He was too angry to speak.

Terel had no such problem. She wept into a lace-trimmed hankie. "I am the laughingstock of Chandler. My own sister cavorting about with that man. Where did you spend the night, Nellie? With him?"

Guilt seeped through Nellie with every word they

spoke. If either of them had disappeared for an entire night, she would have been sick with worry. Part of her was glad Jace had destroyed the note or she would not have had the past heavenly twenty-four hours to remember. Another part of her was very sorry to have caused her family so much concern.

"I don't believe you care about us, Nellie," Terel said, sobbing. "You don't care about the misery you caused us."

"Yes, I do," she said meekly.

"But what is to prevent something like this happening again? It seems to me that all Mr. Montgomery has to do is crook his little finger and you come running."

"It's not like that," Nellie said, but she knew that it was. If Jace asked her to leave with him again, she probably would. "I apologize for worrying you. I really do." Tears were coming now. She really had been very inconsiderate in her behavior. "I wish . . ."

"You wish what?" Charles said sternly.

"I wish that both of you got what you wanted from me," she said, and, sobbing, she ran blindly from the room.

Terel and Charles stood staring after her. There was one thing they were in agreement on: What they wanted from Nellie was for her not to interfere with their comfort. If the truth were known, neither of them was too upset over Nellie's absence, but they were furious that their comfort had been disturbed. Charles had had a cold dinner last night, and Terel had returned home to find that her clothes had not been ironed, and today she'd had to cancel her tea party because Nellie had not stayed home to prepare the food for it.

"That's one wish that I hope comes true," Charles muttered.

Terel made her way down Coal Avenue toward her dressmaker's. She had one more fitting for her dress for the Harvest Ball, and then it would be ready. She had spent far too much on the dress, but she'd worry about her father's anger later. She was especially pleased with the gown. It had over a hundred pink silk roses on the skirt and bodice. The short sleeves were layered with lace, and there was a skirt of lace under a draped overskirt of pink silk charmeuse.

She couldn't help smiling as she thought of the entrance she'd make at the Taggerts' on the night of the ball. In fact, she couldn't seem to help smiling about a lot of things. The best, and most surprising, thing was that an invitation to the Harvest Ball had arrived for her after all. She'd been sure that after the little mix-up with those boys last year she'd never be asked back. But Terel guessed that she was so popular now that the Taggerts just couldn't ignore her. In addition, for the last four days Nellie had been a joy. The house had never run more smoothly. The meals had been on time and delicious, and all of Terel's clothes had been perfectly pressed and hung in her wardrobe.

There had been no further mention of the night Nellie had disappeared, and no sign of Mr. Montgomery. After weeks of turmoil it looked as though the

Grayson household was returning to normal. Except that now Terel was indeed the most sought-after young lady in Chandler—she couldn't possibly accept all the invitations extended to her. And her father's business was doing better than it ever had.

An hour later, as Terel stood in front of the mirror in her dressmaker's studio, she looked at herself in her ball gown and smiled. All in all, there wasn't a cloud in her sky.

"Yes, it's perfect," Terel said. "Send it to my house."

The dressmaker was happy to have at last pleased Terel. The many roses had been very time-consuming to make. "Shall I send Nellie's, too?"

Terel stopped pirouetting before the mirror. "Nellie's what?"

"Her dress for the Harvest Ball. Shall I send Nellie's ball gown to your house at the same time I send yours, or would she like to have a final fitting?"

She'd been so busy she'd completely forgotten that Nellie had been invited to the ball as well.

"Let me see the dress," Terel whispered.

"Of course," the dressmaker said, smiling as she stepped behind a curtain into her workroom. "I am very proud of it. I consider it one of my finest creations. I never knew Nellie had such excellent taste in clothes. Of course, the whole town is saying that there is a great deal that they never noticed about Nellie. I for one never realized she was a beauty." She stepped back through the curtain, a gown of ice-blue satin across her arms. "Nellie looks lovely in the dress, really lovely."

The gown was very simple, off the shoulder, low-cut, and Terel knew that Nellie would indeed look lovely in it.

The dressmaker looked at Terel's stricken face. "Have I said something wrong? Perhaps Nellie meant this as a surprise, and now I've spoiled it."

"Yes," Terel said, trying to recover. "I think it was meant to be a surprise. I was hoping Nellie could go to the ball, but I wasn't sure she'd be able to."

"Nellie said something about that. Actually, what she said was quite odd. She said that since both you and your father were going to be out that evening, she didn't think that her going to the ball would disturb your comfort. Wasn't that strange? 'Disturb your comfort.' That's just what she said."

Terel turned away from Nellie's beautiful gown. "Perhaps you'd better send the dresses separately, so when I see Nellie's dress I can be *properly* surprised."

"Yes, of course. That's a good idea."

Later, when Terel was on the street, she knew what she was going to do. She stopped at the five-and-dime and bought a large bag of children's marbles.

Nellie smoothed the ball gown as it draped across her bed. There was a flutter of anticipation inside her as she touched the blue silk. She knew that tonight was going to be very special. For a moment she closed her eyes and imagined waltzing with Jace.

A knock on the door brought her back to reality. Her first thought was to hide her dress, but Terel entered before Nellie could move.

"Nellie, I wondered—" Terel began, but then she saw the gown. "How beautiful, how utterly beautiful." She gave Nellie a look of surprise. "Why, it totally slipped my mind that you are going to the ball tonight, too."

Nellie could feel her face turning red. "Mr. Montgomery invited me, and I thought that since both you and Father would be gone this evening that you wouldn't mind if I went out. I wouldn't stay for the whole ball. I . . ." She could feel her hopes for the evening fade as she saw anger on Terel's face.

"Nellie, you act as though Father and I are monsters, or worse, jailers. I don't like being thought of as an ogre."

"No, of course not. I didn't mean to offend you. I just didn't want to interfere with your . . . your comfort. I don't have to go to the ball. I can—"

Terel took a few steps across the room and kissed Nellie's cheek. "How silly you are. My comfort, indeed. *Your* comfort is what's important." She picked up the gown from the bed. "This is beautiful, and when you're wearing it you will be beautiful also. Oh, Nellie, we'll be the two prettiest girls there."

Nellie smiled. "Do you think so?"

"I'm sure of it." She held the dress up to the light. "This really is the most exquisite silk, and the color is perfect for you. Did you choose it yourself?"

"Yes," Nellie said, beginning to relax, and she wondered what she had been afraid of. She had purposely hidden the dress from Terel, had kept secret the fact that she was going to the ball.

Carefully, so as not to crease the dress, Terel put it across her arms. "We have to get dressed together. I'll help you with your hair, and—Nellie, my opal necklace would look divine with this dress. Come on," she said when she was at the door. "Don't just stand there, we have work to do. Tomorrow everyone in town will be talking about the Grayson girls."

Nellie felt so happy she wanted to cry. What in the world had she been worried about? Smiling, she followed Terel out of the room.

Three hours later Nellie stood before the long mirror in Terel's room. Her dress looked even better than she'd hoped it would, and the opal necklace was perfect with it. Her hair was fuller on one side than the other, and the curls over her forehead were scorched from the curling iron and a little odd-looking, but Terel admitted she wasn't very good with hair. Nellie didn't mind. For the first time Nellie thought the reflection staring back at her was pretty, and, along with feeling that she looked good, Nellie felt warm inside because of the pleasant three hours she had spent with her sister. This afternoon it had seemed like they really were sisters, rather than, as Nellie often felt, mother and daughter. They had arranged each other's hair, pulled each other's corset strings, and profusely admired each other's gowns.

"You'll have to choose fabrics for me," Terel said, looking at Nellie in her cool blue gown. "Maybe you would have chosen a different ball gown for me."

Feeling almost lightheaded with joy over the coming evening and for once not feeling old and frumpy, Nellie spoke before she thought. "Fewer roses and not that shade of pink."

Terel's smile left her face. "Oh?"

Some of Nellie's joy fled. "I'm sorry. I didn't mean that. I just meant that . . ." She couldn't think what to say.

Terel smiled again and sat down at her dressing table. "Perhaps you're right. Next time I want you to choose my dresses for me. Oh my, look at the time! The men will be here soon."

Nellie's breath quickened at just the thought of seeing Jace again.

"Oh, heavens," Terel said, "I've done it again. I've left the cap off the bottle of ink. I was writing thank-you notes and forgot the cap. Nellie, would you hand me the bottle? And be careful, don't spill it."

Smiling, still thinking of Jace, Nellie went to the table by the bed and picked up the bottle of India ink. She did not see Terel open the bag of marbles and dump them on the floor. As they began to roll across the floor Terel covered the noise by going into a coughing fit. Nellie, concerned, ran to her sister. She had not taken three steps before she stepped on a marble and slipped, falling sideways against Terel's bed.

"Nellie!" Terel exclaimed. "Look at you!"

To her horror, Nellie looked down at her beautiful gown, at the ink saturating the skirt. The dress was ruined beyond repair.

"Quick, get it off. We'll soak the ink out and—"

"It's ruined," Nellie whispered, standing, then bending to pick up two marbles.

"Where did they come from?" Terel asked.

"They were on the floor."

Terel put her hand to her mouth in horror. "Oh, no, Nellie, is that what caused you to slip? I bought the marbles to take to the Taggert children. I thought it might help the Taggerts to forgive me for what happened last year. I never thought—"

Terel said more, but Nellie wasn't listening. Part of her was telling herself that she should have known that something would happen to ruin this evening. She had wanted it too much for it to have come about. Another part of her was enraged. How could Terel have done this to her?

"It was an accident," she muttered to herself.

"Of *course* it was an accident," Terel said, indignant. "You don't think that I—that I could have . . ." She put her hands over her face. "Nellie, how could you hate me so much as to think that I could have wanted to ruin your dress? *Why* would I have wanted to hurt you?"

Nellie's anger left her as she hugged Terel. "I'm sorry. Of course it was an accident. Of course you wouldn't have done something like this." She looked down at her dress. Now she wouldn't be able to go to the ball, for she had no other dress at all suitable.

Terel pushed away from Nellie. "We must hurry and find you something else to wear. The men will be here soon."

"I have nothing else," Nellie said tiredly.

"Then you'll have to wear something of mine. You can wear my green gown. The color will look good on you."

Nellie was trying to keep her dignity. "I could not possibly wear one of your dresses. I'm too . . . I'm not your size."

"Oh," Terel said, looking at Nellie. "I don't guess we can even let out the seams enough. We'll just have to borrow a dress. Now, who in town is your size?"

"No one is my size," Nellie said, fighting tears. "No one at all."

"Mrs. Hutchinson," Terel said thoughtfully. "Yes, that's it, we'll go to Mrs. Hutchinson and—"

Mrs. Hutchinson was a horrid old woman who lived on the edge of town. She was three hundred pounds if she was an ounce, and she dressed like a man and smelled like the pigs she raised. It was rumored that in her younger days she had been a mule skinner.

"No," Terel said, "Mrs. Hutchinson would never have a ball gown. But who else in town is as large as you?"

The muscles in Nellie's throat were working as she tried to keep from crying. *Was* she as fat as Mrs. Hutchinson?

Terel put her shoulders back. "I shan't go. If my sister can't go, then I won't either."

Nellie wiped at her eyes with the back of her hand. "That's ridiculous. Of course you'll go."

Terel began picking up marbles from the floor. "No, I won't. What kind of sister would I be if I let you stay here all alone, and besides it was my ink, and I'm the one who bought the marbles. And it was my coughing that must have knocked them off the table. I shouldn't have coughed. I don't know why I've been coughing lately. I must go see Dr. Westfield. I should probably stay home tonight and rest anyway. You and I will make cookies, and you can eat all of them. Yes, Nellie, that's what we'll do. Now, will you help me out of my dress? Anyway, you said it was an ugly dress."

Terel's words made Nellie stop thinking of herself. "Your dress is beautiful, and you are beautiful, and you *must* go to the ball."

"Not without you."

It took Nellie forty-five minutes to persuade Terel to go to the ball without her. Her escort came and had to wait in the parlor for thirty minutes while Nellie tried to persuade Terel to go without her. But at last Terel left with her escort in a swirl of roses and lace and pink silk, and Nellie closed the door behind them.

She was still wearing her blue dress, the ink stain now over most of the skirt. Hunger attacked her, deep, gnawing hunger. She pushed away from the door and started for the kitchen, but a knock on the door halted her. She opened it to see Jace standing there. He wore dark evening clothes, and he looked as handsome as a prince in a fairy tale.

"I'm sorry I'm late," he said, "but there were cows on the railroad track, and the train was delayed, and—Nellie, what's wrong?"

Even as he said it he pulled her into his arms, and her tears, held back for over an hour now, came pouring out. Jace could hardly understand what she was saying. He pulled her head off his shoulder and put his fingers under her chin. "What is this about your not being able to go?"

"My gown is ruined."

He stepped back to look at her skirt. "Your little sister been at it again?"

"Terel didn't do this. She was coughing, and the marbles fell, and I—"

"Uh-huh. Sure." He pulled out his handkerchief and wiped Nellie's eyes. "Now, sweetheart, blow your nose, because I have a surprise for you." He stepped back to reveal two people behind him, a man and a woman. The man's arms were full of boxes, and the woman carried a little leather case. Nellie looked at Jace questioningly.

"This is Houston's maid, and she's come to do your hair." He looked at the curls on Nellie's head. "Did Terel burn yours?"

"She didn't mean to, she—"

"And the man has a few pieces of clothing for you."

"Clothing? I don't understand."

"Go upstairs and let Elsie get you dressed. I can explain everything later. Your sister *is* gone, isn't she? I don't want ink on this dress, and I don't want her burning your hair off."

"Terel didn't—"

"Scoot!" he ordered, and Nellie obeyed him, hurrying up the stairs, the two servants behind her.

Houston's maid was quick, efficient, and very good with hair. "Such beautiful, thick hair," she said as she coiled Nellie's hair expertly and pinned it into place. "And what perfect skin!"

Nellie felt herself blushing under the woman's compliments. It was when she saw the dress that Nellie was speechless.

"We must remove your ruined gown and—"

"I can't wear that," Nellie gasped. "It's too beautiful for me." The dress was of a heavenly silver satin and it was embroidered all over the skirt with seed pearls. The low, square-cut bodice had sleeves of silver lace. It was the most exquisite, divinely beautiful dress Nellie had ever seen.

Houston's maid didn't put up with Nellie's hesitations. Within minutes she had Nellie out of her ruined dress and into the silver one. Nellie stood before the mirror looking at herself. She could not believe that the reflection she was seeing was her own.

"And now for the jewels," Elsie said. She fastened a necklace of three tiers of diamonds around Nellie's neck, and then more diamonds in her ears. Three diamond clusters went into Nellie's hair.

"Is that me?" Nellie whispered at the mirror.

"Stunning," Elsie said, smiling. "You will be the most beautiful girl there."

Nellie looked away from the mirror. "I am not a girl, and, at this size, I am not beautiful."

"Mr. Montgomery doesn't seem to believe anything is wrong with your size."

"He doesn't, does he?" Nellie said in wonder, looking back at the mirror. Tonight she could almost believe that she wasn't an old maid, wasn't a fat woman past her prime.

"That's better," Elsie said, laughing. "I hope you have a wonderful time tonight."

"I do, too." Nellie smiled and thought of Terel. Now Terel wouldn't have to feel bad about the accident with the ink.

Downstairs, any doubts she had about the way she looked vanished when she saw Jace. For the first time in her life Nellie experienced how beautiful a woman can feel when her beauty is reflected in a man's eyes. Jace looked at her with some awe, and Nellie felt herself change. She swept down the stairs, basking in Jace's admiration.

"Are those flowers for me?" she asked when she was standing before him. He was gaping at her, unable to say a word.

Nellie laughed and took the flowers from his hand as Elsie slipped a mink cape about Nellie's shoulders.

"Go on," Elsie said, urging them out the door.

In the carriage, driving up to the Taggerts' house, Jace kept looking at her as though he'd never seen her before. By the time they reached the ball, Nellie was feeling as though maybe Elsie had been right—as though she was the most beautiful woman in the world.

They were the last ones to arrive at the ball, and

when a footman started to help Nellie off with her cloak Jace possessively pushed him away.

"You are the most beautiful woman I've ever seen in my life," Jace whispered. "I'm not sure I want any other men to look at you."

Nellie smiled at him. "I'm sure you're the only man here who will think a fat old maid like me is pretty," she said, but for the first time she didn't believe the words. Tonight, in this dress, she didn't feel fat or old.

Inside the ballroom, other men looked at Nellie in much the same way that Jace had.

"Is that Nellie Grayson?" one man asked.

"That is Terel's sister?"

"Terel who?"

Laughing, the men descended on Nellie and Jace.

"Well?" Houston asked her husband Kane as he stared at Nellie. "What was it you said about 'fat ladies'?"

Kane grinned. "There's fat and there's fat. She looks like a peach, as plump and as ripe as a peach."

Houston slipped her arm through her husband's. "Knowing your love for peaches, I think I'd as soon you stayed away from Nellie."

He smiled down at his wife. "I'll bet that little sister of hers ain't gonna like Nellie's looks."

"I fear not," Houston said softly.

It took Terel a while to realize that her audience of adoring men was leaving her. Since she'd arrived, she'd been the most popular girl in the room. She had been swamped with invitations for dances, and for social events in the coming weeks. She had sat on a lovely gilt chair and held court with all the condescension of a princess talking to her subjects. Louisa, Charlene, and Mae had stood together in a corner and given Terel looks of rage. Each look had made Terel feel even better.

Six men had left before she realized the numbers were dwindling. She saw one very handsome man punch another and motion with his head. Both men disappeared into the crowd. Terel looked at Charlene and saw that she, too, was looking toward the center of the room.

Terel stopped fluttering her fan and, as the music stopped and the dancers drew aside, she saw what everyone was looking at. In the center of the room, wearing a dress that any woman would sell her soul for, was Nellie. Only this Nellie, with her head up, with diamonds flashing off her body, with a smile of happiness on her beautiful face, was not the Nellie who washed and ironed clothes. *This* Nellie was altogether different.

She was looking up at Jace Montgomery, and Terel saw that he was even better-looking than usual, and he was looking at Nellie as no man had ever looked at Terel.

Terel clenched her fists so hard, her nails cut into her palms.

"Who would have thought," Charlene whispered, "that your competition would come from your own sister?" She was very angry at Terel's recent and inexplicable popularity.

"Doesn't Nellie look nice?" Mae said. "I've never seen her look so pretty. Where do you think she got that dress?"

Terel began to realize that people were looking at her. She forced a smile, then stood and made her way toward Nellie.

"Terel," Nellie said, kissing her sister's cheek, "I was able to come after all."

Terel looked at the diamonds around Nellie's throat and in her ears, and at the pearls on her dress. "I'm so very glad. Did a man buy you that dress?" There was an insinuation in her voice that Nellie had traded "favors" for the dress.

"I gave Nellie the dress," Houston said before Nellie could speak, and she gave Terel a hard look.

Terel was aware of people watching her, as though daring her to say or do something.

"May I have this dance?" Jace asked Nellie. He didn't give Terel a chance to say another word before he swept her away.

After that, the ball lost all excitement for Terel. Nothing meant anything to her—not the invitations she received, not the compliments of the men— nothing. She could not take her eyes off Nellie. How? Terel thought. How could someone as fat and as boring as Nellie cause so much interest? Nearly everyone at the ball was swarming around Nellie. There were young men around Terel, yes, but there were no women, neither young nor old.

But everyone was speaking to Nellie. Old women,

young women, men, even the Taggert children, allowed into the ball for a few minutes, went to see their Cousin Jace and ended by kissing Nellie good night. Terel grimaced when she heard the oohs from people at the children's kissing of Nellie.

Nellie's presence might have been bearable if it had been only older people paying attention to her, but it was the men's attention that infuriated Terel. All the *boys* asked Terel to dance, but all the *men* asked Nellie to dance. She saw Dr. Westfield dancing with Nellie, then laughing uproariously at something she said. Edan Nylund and Rafe Taggert, men who'd never so much as looked at Terel, asked Nellie to dance.

"I never looked at Nellie before," the young man dancing with Terel said. "I guess I thought she was old, and maybe a little—well—fat, but she doesn't look fat tonight. She moves like a goddess."

Terel stopped dancing and left the man standing alone on the dance floor. She left the ballroom and went outside into the cool night air.

"Couldn't bear to see how much people like Nellie?"

She jumped, then turned to see Jace standing in the shadows. "I have no idea what you mean, Mr. Montgomery. I am very pleased to see my sister so happy."

"You're not pleased to see anyone have more than you do."

"I'll not stand here and be insulted like this." She started to go back to the ballroom, but Jace caught her arm.

"I know what you're up to, you don't fool me one bit. You're a spoiled brat who's had everything given to her all her life, and you think Nellie was put on this earth to give to you. Tonight you're eaten alive with jealousy because you know that everyone in there *likes* Nellie, and you know that not one of them likes you."

She jerked her arm from his grasp. "You should talk of liking! All you want from my old maid sister is our father's money. I am merely trying to protect my sister from—" She stopped because Jace was laughing at her.

"Your father's money," he said with a sneer. "Before you go accusing people you should do a little research. I want Nellie because she's everything a woman should be—everything that you're not." He leaned over Terel in a threatening way. "I'm warning you, you'd better leave Nellie alone. No more ink on her dresses, no more telling her she's fat. You understand me? You keep making her cry and you'll have to answer to me."

At that he turned and walked back into the ballroom.

For a while Terel was too stunned to move. No one had ever talked to her like that before, and as she watched him go to Nellie and saw the two of them start dancing together Terel's anger turned to something deeper. Research, he'd said, and he'd said it as though there was something she should know about him.

She went back to the ballroom and began to ask questions. It didn't take many questions to find out that Jace Montgomery was one of the heirs to Warbrooke Shipping. Terel had no doubt that her father knew all about Warbrooke Shipping, and that that was why he'd hired Jace in the first place—and the man had accepted employment just to be near Nellie.

As Terel danced and smiled and chatted her mind worked. Under no circumstances on earth was she going to allow her fat, old-maid sister to catch one of the richest men in America. Was she, Terel, to marry some boy from Chandler and settle for a small house while Nellie lived in a mansion in New York? Or Paris? Or wherever she wanted to live? Was she supposed to spend her life reading about Nellie in the society pages of the newspaper? Maybe Nellie would feel sorry for her little sister's poverty and send Terel her cast-off clothing. Was Nellie to have everything that Terel wanted in life just because she happened to meet Jace Montgomery first? If Terel had gone down first to greet the man that night he came to dinner, no doubt he'd be in love with her now.

She is taking everything that *should* have been mine, Terel thought. My own sister has betrayed me by taking everything I've ever wanted.

Well, she can't have it, Terel thought. What is mine is mine, and she can't take it away from me.

She looked at Nellie, standing near Jace, drinking a cup of punch and listening to Kane Taggert. The man had never so much as given the time of day to Terel.

"I'll get her," Terel whispered. "If I die trying, I'll keep her from taking what's mine."

She turned away from Nellie and smiled at the young man near her. For all the world she seemed to be enjoying herself, but in her mind she was concocting a plan.

Chapter Eight

THE KITCHEN

*B*erni stepped out of the bathtub and once again looked at her list. She didn't know how long she'd been in the Luxury room, but it was long enough to have chosen three things from the list.

After having given Nellie her three wishes, Berni entered the Luxury room and was given a long list of pleasures from which to choose. Since she'd spent the previous fourteen years partying, the first thing she chose from the list was "videos."

Following golden lights through the fog, she entered an enormous room filled with shelves of videos of every movie ever made, plus every episode of every TV show. She had merely to look at the titles and they were chosen for her. After choosing a few hundred movies and old TV shows—everything Mary Tyler

Moore had ever done and all the early "Bonanza" episodes—she followed the lights to a beautiful bedroom. The bed, covered with two-hundred-and-fifty-dollar sheets and pillowcases trimmed with handmade lace, was high off the floor and as soft as down (there were no "good for you" orthopedic mattresses in the Kitchen). She lay in bed for a very long while, eating endless bowls of buttery popcorn and watching one video after another. She didn't even have to get out of bed to change the tapes, and when Mel Gibson was kissing someone the tape automatically slowed its speed.

After many, many videos she got out of bed and looked at her list. The next luxury she chose was "friendships with women." On earth Berni had never had any women friends, but she had always heard and even believed that other women had solid, loving friendships with each other. So, for a long period of time, Berni had women friends. They went shopping together, giggled together, had lunch. Her friends gave her a birthday party, and they were always there to listen to her. When one of her friends broke up with her boyfriend, Berni stayed up all night with her.

But Berni grew tired of listening to other people, so she looked at her list again. This time she chose "bubble bath." She sat in a large, soft bathtub full of hot water and lots of bubbles, read trashy novels, ate chocolate-covered cherries, and drank pink champagne. The water never grew cold; the bubbles never burst; the books were always good and the candy and champagne delicious.

Now, leaving the tub, she was looking at her list again. "New clothes" intrigued her. On earth she'd realized that the only clothes she really liked to wear were new ones. She would have liked to wear something only once, then discard it. "Kids who behave like those on TV" also interested her. There was also "winning prizes" and "being popular in high school" and "being appreciated."

She was trying to decide when Pauline walked into the bathroom. As soon as Berni saw her the bathroom disappeared, and Berni was once again wearing the suit in which she'd been buried.

"You must come with me," Pauline said sternly. "There is a problem in the Grayson household."

Berni gave a grimace, then followed Pauline through the fog. She hadn't thought of that fatty, Nellie, since she'd given her three wishes. "What's she done? Wished her little sister into the grave?"

Pauline didn't reply until they were in the Viewing Room; then she waved her hand and the fog cleared. Berni could see a cutaway of the Grayson house, rather like a doll house, with the upstairs and the downstairs showing at once. Terel was in the parlor, beautifully dressed, entertaining half a dozen equally well-dressed friends with tea and cakes. Charles was in the dining room with four men, looking at plans for a new freight office. The men were drinking whiskey and eating thick roast beef sandwiches. Nellie was running from the kitchen to the parlor to the dining room, trying to obey every demand her sister and father made.

Berni looked at the scene and frowned. "Can I help it if she didn't take her wishes? It's not my fault if she's too dumb to—"

"Nellie made her wishes, she just wished for things for other people."

"For other people? How can you make a wish for someone else?"

Pauline looked back at the house. "Nellie's first wish was given to her sister. Terel said she wanted to be the most popular girl in town, so Nellie wished it for her. Of course, Nellie has had to cook and clean and take care of Terel's wardrobe due to her little sister's new popularity."

Pauline turned to look at Berni. "Nellie's second wish was that her father's business would become more successful. It has, but, as you can see, Nellie has had even more work dumped on her shoulders."

"They're big enough to handle it," Berni muttered. "What was her third wish?"

"It was an unusual wish, actually. She wished that her father and sister would get what they wanted from her. What they wanted was that Nellie not interfere with their comfort."

"Their comfort?"

"Yes," Pauline said. "Nellie's third wish has made her virtually a slave to her father and sister. She can't leave the house unless she's sure it won't interfere with the ease of her family. Look at her." Pauline turned back to the screen. "She's much worse off now than she was to begin with. At least she had free choice before you gave her the wishes."

Berni watched Nellie scurrying from room to room, both her sister and her father hissing at her that she wasn't moving quickly enough. In the kitchen, when Nellie wasn't there, Berni could see the maid Anna sneaking in and stealing food to give to a disreputable-looking boyfriend who hid outside. When Nellie was in the kitchen she would call for Anna, but the maid would hide and giggle.

"Why didn't she use her wishes for herself?" Berni asked. "She could have had anything."

"You didn't let her know she had three wishes, and you said her wishes were for what she *really wanted*. Nellie wants other people to be happy."

Berni frowned. "What happened to the hunk?"

"He's still around, and he's in love with Nellie, but I'm afraid something is going to happen."

"Such as?"

"Yesterday there was a ball, and Nellie looked lovely. It made Terel very jealous, and—"

"Jealous? Pretty little Terel was jealous of a blimp like Nellie?"

"There is more to a person than fat," Pauline said. "Everyone in town likes Nellie, and they are happy to see her looking pretty and with a man like Mr. Montgomery. For all Terel's prettiness, she isn't nice like Nellie is."

Berni looked away. On earth there had been times in her life when she'd been eaten alive with jealousy, and it hadn't been the beauty queens who'd made her jealous but women like—well, like Nellie—who seemed to inspire love wherever they went.

"So what do I do now?" Berni asked softly. "Give her more wishes? Can I override the wishes she messed up?"

"No. What's done is done. You have to figure out how to help Nellie. It's up to you."

A new emotion was creeping into Berni. It was guilt. She'd bragged to Pauline that she'd never hurt anyone in her life, at least not anyone who hadn't done something rotten to her. But this Nellie hadn't done anything to Berni, yet she'd managed to genuinely harm her.

"Can I see what's gone on since I last saw Nellie?"

"Of course." Pauline waved her hand, and the screen changed back to that evening when Jace Montgomery had first come to dinner.

Berni settled down on a banquette and watched. She saw Jace persuade Nellie to walk out with him, saw him help her up on the wall, saw the way Nellie's face lit when Jace touched her.

"And she doesn't even know he's rich," Berni murmured. She saw Terel when she heard the news of Nellie's having spent the day with Jace. Berni winced when she heard and saw the way Charles and Terel berated Nellie for having spent a day out.

"They're only worried because Nellie didn't fix dinner for them," Berni muttered.

"What?" Pauline asked.

"I said they don't care about Nellie, only about themselves."

"How do you know that?"

WISHES

"Because I—" Berni stopped, and her voice lowered. "Because I've done the same thing to my sister. All I had to do was tell her she was selfish and she'd do *anything* I wanted." Berni looked back at the screen. "If only Nellie were thin . . ."

"How would that help?"

"I don't know, but I'm sure all her problems come from her being fat."

"I'm not sure you're right. Maybe when you see all of what's happened, see when Nellie gives her wishes away and—"

She broke off because a woman ran into the room. "A ship's gone down!"

"Oh, my," Pauline said, smiling.

"What's happened?" Berni asked.

The new woman, who wore ancient Egyptian dress, her black hair coated with oil, looked very excited. "A ship has gone down in 1742. All hands went down with it."

Pauline stood. "I must go. This doesn't happen very often, and—well, I don't want to miss it. You stay and watch Nellie."

"Wait a minute." Berni caught Pauline's arm. "Explain what's going on."

"The men went down with the ship. There are usually hundreds of them, and they're young and healthy, and they've been at sea sometimes for a year or more. Alone. With no women."

Berni was beginning to understand. "You mean that a few hundred—"

161

"Two hundred and thirty-six," the Egyptian woman said.

"Two hundred and thirty-six lonely young sailors are coming to the Kitchen?"

"Exactly," Pauline said.

"So when I get through watching Nellie I can—"

"There are no men allowed in the Kitchen, remember? Not *real* men, anyway. There are men in some of the rooms, but they're actually just images. These men are *real.*"

Berni thought of all the things she liked about men, the way they laughed and strutted, the way men could make you feel gorgeous, the way they could make you feel rotten and wonderful at the same time. "Real men," Berni said dreamily.

"Yes." Pauline smiled. "When a ship goes down or a mine explodes, or there's some other natural disaster where a lot of men are killed, sometimes they're sent here before being sent on to heaven or hell. They're only here a few hours and then they're gone. If you want to visit with them, you have to go *now.*"

Berni looked back at the screen. Nellie was in the kitchen, her arm extended into the pantry, and that gorgeous Jace Montgomery was hungrily kissing her. Berni didn't think Nellie looked too bad off. If only she weren't so fat . . .

"Let's go to the sailors," Berni said.

"But what about Nellie?"

Berni waved her arm. "Get skinny, kid." She looked back at Pauline. "That should do it. She gets skinny and she won't have a problem in her life."

"I'm not so sure. Maybe you should stay and—"

"Come on," the Egyptian woman said. "The men will all be claimed by the time we get there."

"Don't worry," Berni said to Pauline. "Nellie will be fine. She'll be thin and beautiful, and all her problems will be solved. Now let's go."

After a moment's hesitation, Pauline lifted her long skirts and started running after Berni and the Egyptian woman.

CHANDLER, COLORADO
1896

Jace was roused from sleep by someone pounding on the door of his hotel room. He struck a match, lit the lamp by the bed, and looked at his pocket watch. Three-thirty A.M. "All right, I'm coming," he called, pulling on his trousers, buttoning them as he went to the door. He opened it to see a boy standing there, a thick kid of about ten or eleven.

"I got a telegram for you," the boy said.

Rubbing his eyes sleepily, Jace took the telegram and looked at it.

YOUR FATHER GRAVELY ILL STOP COME HOME AT ONCE

Jace read it three times before his thoughts began to clear. "When's the next train east?"

"There's one at four, but it's a freight train. Don't take fancy passengers."

Jace's mind was racing. "Come here," he told the boy. He went to the little desk in the room, sat down, and began to write a note to Nellie. He explained where he was going and why. He told her he'd return as soon as possible and asked her to explain to her father. At the bottom of the letter he told her he loved her.

Jace stood, sealed the letter in an envelope, addressed it to Nellie, then turned to the boy. "Do you know Miss Nellie Grayson?"

"Everybody knows Nellie."

"I want you to give this to her. To her and no one else, you understand me?"

"Sure thing, mister."

Jace pulled a quarter from his pocket. It was too much to give to the boy, but he wanted to insure his loyalty. "To Nellie and no one else."

"I heard you the first time."

"Go," Jace said. "I have to pack." The boy left, and Jace threw some clothes into a bag. He meant to make the four A.M. train. Even if he had to ride on top of a coal car, he was going to be on the first transportation out of Chandler. When he snapped his bag shut he paused. His father ill. His robust, aggressively healthy father ill. As he picked up his bag his hand trembled a bit.

There was no one downstairs at the hotel desk, so he quickly wrote a note saying he was checking out, then left money with the note. When that was done he began running. He made it to the train station as fast as his long legs could travel, and once there he paid an exorbitant amount for passage inside a freight car to Denver. He didn't care what discomfort he had to endure. He was going to get to Maine and his father as fast as possible.

"Well?" Terel demanded of the boy. Last summer she had seen the boy terrorizing a little girl half his size and age, and she knew that he would be the one to do what she wanted.

"I done it." The boy squinted his eyes at her. "He give me two bits."

"You little blackmailer," Terel muttered. She'd promised the boy to double whatever Jace gave him if he'd bring her any note Jace might write. She gave the kid fifty cents, taking Jace's note at the same time. "One word of this gets out and I'll know who told," she said, threatening him.

"You can do your own sister in for all I care," the boy said, backing away from her and grinning insolently. "You need any more help, Duke's the one."

She glared at him, refusing to call him by his self-given name of Duke. "I won't need you anymore. Go home."

He grinned again, then took off running.

Terel shivered in the cold morning and could feel that the crisp, pretty days were almost over and winter would be there soon. She lifted her ball gown off the gravel and started to walk home. She hadn't been home since yesterday, the night of the Harvest Ball, the night that had come so close to changing her life.

She crumpled the letter Jace had written and kept walking. It would take him weeks to get to Maine and back, and by the time he returned Terel planned to have Nellie convinced that Jace Montgomery was a blackguard, and that he'd deserted her. She smiled in the gray early-morning light and quickened her step. Today she was having a tea party for her friends so they could discuss the ball. She planned to have some extraordinary gossip for them.

Nellie awoke with a start, and at first she thought that last night had been a dream, but as her eyes focused she saw her beautiful gown hanging on the back of the door. For a few moments of luxury she closed her eyes and relived last night. Being in Jace's arms. Seeing him smile at her, his dimple showing now and then. She remembered feeling so proud: proud of him, proud of herself, proud just to be alive. He'd kissed her when he brought her home, kissed her and told her he loved her.

Nellie hadn't said anything in return. What she was feeling for Jace was more than love; it was closer to worship. He was changing how she felt about herself, how she looked at the world. He was changing how the entire town looked at her, spoke to her, thought of her. Love him? she thought. What she felt for him was considerably more than love.

Slowly, Nellie got out of bed and began to dress. She felt almost dreamy after last night. Even though she'd had only a few hours sleep she felt wonderful. For a moment she waltzed about the room in her underwear.

She stopped and smiled. "You great cow," she said, but with no real anger in her voice. "Stop daydreaming and get to work." She picked up her corset, slipped it on over her head, and then started pulling the front drawstrings closed.

"That's odd," she said aloud. Usually she had to pull the strings hard to make the sides come within four inches of meeting, but this morning the sides of the corset were only two inches apart. She pulled on her old brown dress. Yesterday the dress had been so tight the ribs in her corset could be seen, but today the dress was almost loose.

Nellie smiled. "Probably all the dancing last night," she said, then hurried from the room.

For the rest of the day she had no more time to think, for there was an enormous amount of work to do. Her father was talking to investors, and she had to prepare food for them. Terel was having some of her women friends over for tea, and there were cakes to bake and ice.

By three P.M. she was already exhausted. She hadn't had a moment to sit down, but she hadn't stopped smiling all day. For once in her life it seemed she had pleased everyone. At breakfast her father had beamed at her, said he had heard she'd taken Mr. Montgomery's eye. He said some things about ships that Nellie didn't understand, but she'd been too busy serving buttermilk biscuits to ask questions. Later she'd overheard her father say to Terel, "If Montgomery wants her, he can have her. I can hire a housekeeper for what the man will bring this family."

"If Montgomery wants her," Nellie had whispered, and she felt her skin glow with warmth as she carried a platter of ham into the dining room.

All day Terel had been especially kind to her. Terel had talked of their going to dances together in the future, of their shopping together and maybe even getting married in a joint ceremony.

Marriage, Nellie had thought as she rolled out pastry for apple tarts. Terel was smiling at her from across the big work table. "I'm not sure Mr. Montgomery has marriage in mind. Perhaps he . . ." Children of her own, she thought. A home of her own.

"You couldn't see the way he looked at you. Oh, Nellie, you two looked so good together last night. Hardly anyone remarked on the fact that you're twice as wide as he is."

"Twice as . . ." Nellie ate two slices of apple coated in sugar and cinnamon.

"It didn't matter at all. You just looked divine. I was so proud of you."

Nellie smiled and began placing apple slices on the pastry. "I had a wonderful time."

"Yes, I know you did. When will you see him again?"

"I don't know. Sometimes he comes by in the afternoon." She glanced toward the kitchen door, almost expecting to see him there.

"I'm sure he'll turn up sooner or later. Nellie, I don't mean to pry, but you didn't . . . I mean, well, last night you seemed to be very free with him. Not that I'd ever be one to criticize, but you kept—well, touching him in a very improper way."

"I didn't mean to." Nellie ate four slices of apple.

"No, of course you didn't, and only a few people commented on it, and I'm sure they know you're a woman of good repute. They know you're not the . . . well, the loose woman you seemed to be last night."

On the end of the table there was a large tray covered with freshly baked cookies. Nellie ate two cookies.

"I just wondered," Terel continued, "if you'd allowed him to do anything to you. You are still a virgin, aren't you?"

Nellie ate two more cookies. "I am still a virgin," she whispered.

Terel stood. "Good. I told Father I would ask. He'd heard so much about your behavior last night that he came to me for advice. I assured him that even though you may have looked like a wanton woman I was sure you weren't. Now I can reassure him and everyone else in town." She moved around the table to kiss Nellie's cheek. "You looked so good last night, Nellie. Please remember that and don't eat so many cookies that you won't be able to wear that lovely gown again.

It would be a shame to insult Mrs. Taggert's generosity by gaining even more weight." She smiled. "See you at tea," she said, then she left the room.

Nellie ate two dozen cookies before she could stop herself. *Had* she acted like a wanton woman last night? *Was* the entire town talking about her behavior? She knew how she felt about Jace, but had she actually made a fool of herself before everyone?

When she pulled three dozen petit fours from the oven she ate a dozen of them before she could get them iced. Now, when she thought of the ball, she saw herself as Terel had described her, "twice as wide as he is," and she saw the townspeople watching her in disbelief as she acted like a harlot.

She had to make a second batch of icing for the little cakes because she ate the first bowlful.

"Terel, what is it?" Mae asked, watching Terel sniff prettily into her handkerchief.

Eight young women of Chandler were gathered in the Grayson parlor discussing with great enthusiasm the ball of the night before. The main topic of conversation was Nellie and the great change that had taken place.

"I'd never even looked at Nellie before."

"She was so beautiful, and Mr. Montgomery looked at her with such love in his eyes. He—"

It was at that point that Terel began to sniff delicately. The young ladies were so engrossed in their conversation that it was a while before Mae noticed and asked Terel what was wrong.

"It's nothing," Terel said. "At least it's nothing I can share with anyone outside my family."

Charlene looked at Louisa. "We've known you all your life. We are very close to being family."

Terel touched her handkerchief to the corner of her eye. "You'll all know sooner or later anyway."

"Sooner, preferably," Mae said, but Charlene elbowed her in the ribs.

"Mr. Montgomery is a . . ."

They all waited, leaning forward on their chairs, cups suspended in midair.

"He's a gigolo!"

"No," three women breathed.

"I'm afraid it's true," Terel said, looking very sad. "I was afraid of this from the beginning. It seems that all Mr. Montgomery ever wanted was to buy Grayson Freight."

"But I heard he was rich," Mae said.

"Oh, yes, he is, but don't the rich always want to get richer? Look at Mr. Kane Taggert."

The women looked at each other and nodded in agreement.

"I never trusted him from the first," Terel said. "From the first night he came to dinner I felt uneasy around him. I'm sure he sensed it, so he started courting my poor, dear sister. Poor, poor Nellie. She doesn't have any idea men like that even exist. Nellie is such a sweet, naïve dear, and for the first time in her life a man was paying attention to her. I hadn't the heart to tell her what I thought of Mr. Montgomery. Besides, I could have been wrong."

Terel paused to sniff some more.

"Your instincts were right," Louisa said.

"But last night," Mae said, "he seemed to like Nellie so much. He seemed to adore her. I've never seen a man look at a woman like that."

"Mr. Montgomery should have been on the stage," Terel snapped. "At about nine o'clock I stepped outside for a bit of air—all my many dancing partners were leaving me breathless—and who should be on the porch but Mr. Montgomery?"

"What did he do?" Mae gasped.

"He kissed me!"

"No," all the women said together.

"How dreadful for you."

"How frightful."

"The cad!"

"The scoundrel!"

"I wish he wanted to buy *my* father's business," Mae said dreamily, but she straightened herself when the others glared at her.

"It was what I suspected all along," Terel said. "My father refused to sell his business, and I guess when Mr. Montgomery found that out he tried to obtain the business another way, by courting Nellie."

"I did wonder," Louisa said, "why a man who looks like he does would want a woman like . . . I mean, not that Nellie doesn't have a pretty face, but she is a bit . . . well . . ."

"You don't have to be tactful," Terel said. "Father and I faced the truth a long time ago. Nellie is fat, and she is getting fatter every day. It has been a burden

Father and I have always had to bear. We've tried everything. Both of us have tried to talk to her. Three years ago Father sent her to a clinic outside Denver. She lost some weight while she was there, but as soon as she was home she gained it all back. We just don't know what to do with her. She eats whole cakes and pies, dozens of cookies at a time. It's like a disease with her. We don't know what to do about her." Terel buried her face in her handkerchief.

"We had no idea you had kept such a heavy secret," Charlene said, patting Terel's shoulder.

"You haven't heard half of it."

The women leaned forward again.

"This morning Mr. Montgomery left town on the four A.M. freight train. He checked out of the hotel, no forwarding address, no message to anyone. He just left before daylight. He . . . he . . . oh, I can't say it."

"We're your friends," Charlene said, and Louisa nodded in agreement.

"I think Mr. Montgomery realized that he was not going to get Father's business, and I think he . . . he had his way with Nellie."

The women gasped as one.

"He . . ."

"She . . ."

"They . . ."

"Is she . . . will she have a baby?" Mae whispered, not really knowing the technical aspect of what Nellie was believed to have done, but her mother had warned her emphatically about men and babies.

"I don't know," Terel said into her handkerchief.

"What am I going to do? Father has asked me to be the one to tell Nellie that her . . . her lover has left town. How can I tell her? She is so enamored of the cad that she will never believe anything I say. I'm sure that if I told her about Mr. Montgomery's kissing me she would undoubtedly think it was sisterly jealousy."

"How awful for you," Louisa said. "Surely Nellie would believe her own sister over the word of a stranger."

"If Mr. Montgomery told me the sky was purple, I'd believe him, and nothing my sisters could say would change my mind," Mae said. When the others glared at her, she glared right back.

"Mae is right," Terel said. "You all saw Nellie last night. She believes herself in love with the scoundrel. She'll never believe anything *I* say." She looked over her hankie at the women and waited. Idiots, she thought. Use what limited brainpower you have.

"I shall tell Nellie he also kissed me," Charlene said, looking for all the world like a martyr about to die for a true cause.

"And so shall I," Louisa said with just as much pride.

"I shall say I am carrying his child," Mae whispered, then opened her eyes. "All right. Just one kiss."

"You are such good, dear friends, and someday Nellie will appreciate what you're doing for her."

"We are Nellie's friends, too, and we'll do anything we can to help, but Terel, I was wondering—just because we might need to know, in case Nellie should ask—what was Mr. Montgomery's kiss like?" Charlene asked.

"Yes, purely for the sake of research, perhaps you should tell us," Louisa said.

"Well," Terel began, "just for research, I'd say it was divine. He is a very strong man, and he pulled me quite close to him, and—oh, heavens! I think Mae has fainted."

Chapter Nine

Jace didn't come to visit her the day after the ball, and Nellie tried not to be disappointed. She told herself she was expecting too much, and that perhaps he had business elsewhere. By the second day, when she still hadn't seen him, she decided to make a trip to Randolph's Grocery and perhaps stop by her father's offices to see if Jace was there. She baked six dozen oatmeal-raisin cookies to take to her father's employees.

After what Terel had said about Nellie's conduct the night of the ball, Nellie hadn't ventured out of the house. She was afraid people might look at her oddly, might question her behavior of that night. She knew that seeking out Jace was probably the worst thing she could do for her reputation, but it had been so long since she'd seen him. Also, she wanted to stop by her dressmaker's and see about having a new dress made. For some reason her old dresses didn't seem to fit.

The moment she stepped onto the boardwalk she knew her worst fears had come true. A couple of young men passed her, tipped their hats, then leered at her. Nellie turned away. She waved to three young women across the street, but they pointedly looked away, refusing to acknowledge Nellie's existence.

It is worse than Terel said, Nellie thought. I made a fool of myself before the whole town. And now I'm once again flinging myself at him, she thought. She told herself that under no circumstances should she go to visit Jace, but she kept walking toward her father's office.

As soon as she entered she saw that no one was sitting at Jace's desk. She tried not to look at the empty space, tried not to watch every doorway. She smiled and passed out cookies and asked pleasant questions of each of her father's employees. She was aware of the cautious way they looked at her. Even though they hadn't been at the ball they had obviously heard about her conduct.

She stayed at the freight office for as long as she politely could, then left. No one had even mentioned Jace. She started for the grocery, but Miss Emily saw her from a distance and came running.

"Nellie," Miss Emily said, "I want to talk to you."

Nellie blushed. "I apologize for my behavior," she whispered. "I never meant to embarrass people."

"I just want you to know that I don't believe any of it. That young man really cares for you."

"Yes, I think he does, but that doesn't excuse my conduct."

"We all make mistakes. Now," Miss Emily said, "we have to be practical. What are you going to do about the child?"

"What child?"

"You don't have to pretend with me. Everyone in town knows you're carrying his child. You just have to decide what to do now."

Nellie had to get her mouth closed. "I'm not carrying a child."

"But I heard—" Miss Emily stopped. "Don't tell me this is all gossip! Everyone is saying that that Montgomery fellow was told you were expecting his child and that's why he left town."

Nellie blinked. "Left town? Who left town?"

Miss Emily took a deep breath. "You poor child. What in the world are the gossipmongers of this town doing to you? You'd better come to my house and have a talk."

It was an hour later when Nellie left Miss Emily's house. She didn't feel anything at the moment; her pain was too deep for feeling. Miss Emily had repeated what she had been told by the young ladies who came to her shop. It seemed that while Jace had been visiting Nellie he had also been visiting other women on a regular basis. At least five women told lurid stories of Jace Montgomery's kissing them.

179

Mae Sullivan went into such detail about Mr. Montgomery's touching her that three young ladies had nearly swooned.

"If just one girl had said these things I wouldn't believe her, but it seems that your Mr. Montgomery cut a wide swath through this town. Oh, Nellie, I am so sorry. I usually consider myself a good judge of character, and I thought this man was a gentleman, but it seems that he was not. I've been told he only wanted your father's freight office, and when he couldn't have it he left town." That wasn't the only reason she'd heard he'd left town, Miss Emily thought. If he was as bad as the town was saying and he had had his way with Nellie, time would tell if she carried his child. It was no use making Nellie feel worse than she already did.

"I do believe he cared for you," Miss Emily said, pressing Nellie's hand. "Even if he has turned out to be a base fellow, I am sure he cared for you. He—"

"I must go," Nellie had said, and without another word she left. Once on the street she started toward home. If people snubbed her, she didn't notice.

But she didn't make it home. Instead, she stopped in the bakery and bought doughnuts, fried pies, cookies, cupcakes, cream-filled pastries, and a large chocolate cake. She ignored the look of the woman behind the counter, took the two large bags, and left the store. She didn't think about what she was doing or where she was going; she just started walking.

When at last she stopped walking she was in Fenton Park, in the exact spot where she and Jace had sat and he'd put his head in her lap. She sat on the ground, opened the bags, and began to eat. She tasted nothing, chewed very little, but slowly and systematically ate her way through the first bag.

The tears began when the first bag was emptied. She wasn't really crying; it was just that tears were streaming down her face.

By the middle of the second bag she was so stuffed with food that she had to stretch out on the grass in order to be able to continue eating.

Carrying his child, she thought. No, she wasn't carrying his child. He hadn't quite been able to force himself to go that far to get her father's business. He'd only been able to bring himself to kiss her, to touch her now and then, and to lie to her.

No, she wasn't carrying a child, but Nellie knew she was a woman. She was a woman who had been used by a man, had been used and discarded. She thought of the way she'd believed in him, trusted him, the way she'd given him her love, and again hunger overwhelmed her.

She remembered the night of the Harvest Ball. Miss Emily had said that Jace kissed Terel that night, and he'd kissed Mae and Louisa that night also. Nellie pictured herself with Jace. "Twice as wide," Terel had said. Everyone in town must have been laughing at her as she waltzed with him, he so tall and handsome, she so fat and dumpy. Everyone must have enjoyed the joke greatly. They all must have known why Jace had been courting her. Everyone except Nellie knew. Her father and Terel had tried to warn her, but Nellie hadn't listened. Instead of listening she'd been defiant, believing she knew more about the man than anyone else did.

It was nearly sunset when she picked up her empty bags and started home. On the way she stopped in Randolph's and placed a grocery order for enough food to feed six families for four months.

"Having company?" Mr. Randolph asked, but Nellie didn't answer. She didn't feel like talking or thinking or even living. The only thing she was aware of was a deep, insatiable hunger.

At home her father complained about dinner being late, and Terel wanted to know where Nellie had been, but Nellie didn't answer. She went to the kitchen and began to cook, and for every one thing she cooked and served she cooked two others and ate them. Perhaps her father and Terel talked to her, but she didn't hear them. Her thoughts were completely, totally, absolutely concerned with feeding the hunger that engulfed her.

Nellie ate for three weeks. She didn't care what she ate, when she ate, or how much she ate. Her only concern was in trying to fill up the hunger that ravaged her. Yet no matter how much she ate she still felt empty. It was as though no amount of food in the world could make the hunger go away.

If she stepped into the pantry, where Jace had kissed her and held her, her stomach contracted with hunger. If she looked outside, where the season's first snow now covered her garden, she remembered Jace saying he liked her flowers and she felt ravenous with hunger. If she heard a man laugh, a man speak, if she even saw a man, she was overcome with hunger.

It was Terel who first noticed Nellie's weight loss.

"It can't be because she isn't eating me into bankruptcy," Charles said. "Nellie, this month's grocery bill was enough to break me."

Nellie didn't comment, and her next grocery order was even larger.

"I can't have you looking like this," Charles said after Jace had been gone for four weeks. "You look like a scarecrow. Go get a new dress."

Nellie hadn't bothered to look at herself in a mirror for a long time, but now she did, and she saw that her body was a shadow of its former self. She could hold handfuls of her dress bodice away from her. Reluctantly, not caring what she wore, she went to her dressmaker's.

The dressmaker took one look at Nellie's ravaged face and said not a word. She'd heard all the gossip, of course, and Terel had said that Nellie did nothing but stay home and eat, that she refused to step out of the house, and that her long face was very annoying.

If she's eating, she isn't eating very much, the dressmaker thought as she undressed Nellie down to her smalls. She was amazed that anyone could lose as much weight as Nellie had in such a short time. She went to her workroom to get her tape, but she halted as she looked at a finished gown hanging from a peg in the wall. It was a winter costume she'd just finished for Mrs. Kane Taggert. It was made of dark blue velvet with satin lapels of a lighter blue, and there was a lovely matching cape to the dress.

The dressmaker looked at that velvet gown, knowing that Mr. and Mrs. Taggert would be out of town until after Christmas, and she thought of the way that man had betrayed poor, sweet Nellie. With resolve, she took the dress from its peg, then snatched one of her own corsets from a drawer.

"Now, Nellie, we're going to make you smile."

It took an hour's work to ready Nellie. The dressmaker arranged her hair; since it was dirty, she had to powder it twice to absorb all the oil. She put Nellie into the corset, then hauled on the cords until Nellie's waist was a respectable twenty-one inches, leaving her bosom and hips to swell out above and below her little waist.

Through all of this Nellie stood or sat as commanded, taking very little interest in the proceedings.

The dressmaker got on the telephone and called the milliner. "I want you to bring the blue toque you made for Mrs. Taggert over here. No, she hasn't returned yet, but someone else is here. You'd better come yourself because I don't think you're going to believe this."

When the milliner arrived, indeed, she didn't believe what she saw. She'd known Nellie since she was a pretty little girl, but at twelve, after her mother had died, Nellie had started putting on weight, and her pretty face had been lost atop her big body.

The milliner pushed up her sleeves. "The hair is

wrong. Get a curling iron and call Miss Emily. She should see this."

Thirty minutes later a new Nellie stood before them, hair softly arranged, a fat blue velvet toque jauntily on one side of her head, her hourglass figure encased in a stunning velvet dress. Her beautiful face, with its haunted eyes, looked back at the milliner and seamstress.

When Miss Emily arrived the two women stepped back. No words could describe their achievement, so they just parted and let Miss Emily see their creation. For a moment Miss Emily was speechless. She stood and stared and gaped and gawked. But then she smiled. There was a bit of revenge in that smile. The talk of the treachery of Jace Montgomery had nearly died down in town, but for weeks Miss Emily had had to listen to stories about "poor Nellie." She'd had to hear about how stupid Nellie had been to have believed that a handsome man would like an old maid like her. Well, this vision was no old maid.

"Come with me, Nellie," Miss Emily said firmly. "I mean to show you off."

The seamstress caught Miss Emily's arm. "She hasn't said two words since she arrived. She seems to have been really hurt by that awful man. I'm not sure she realizes she's . . ." She turned and smiled at Nellie. "I'm not sure she knows she's beautiful."

"Once the cats of this town see her they'll let her know," Miss Emily said, then she ushered Nellie out the door.

Nellie was unaware of the sensation she caused as

she walked through Chandler. Men, young and old, stopped to stare. Women did double takes. When Miss Emily escorted Nellie into the tea shop all conversation, all movement, stopped. Miss Emily pushed Nellie forward.

"Mae, Louisa, Charlene," Miss Emily said, "you remember Nellie, don't you?" She got a great deal of pleasure watching the young women's eyes widen. *"Poor* Nellie? Poor, *dear* Nellie?"

"May I have something to eat?" Nellie said softly.

Miss Emily ushered her to a table, and while Nellie had eyes only for the tea cake cart, the young women of Chandler had eyes only for her. Nellie was no longer a person to be pitied, but one to be envied.

Later, after eating a tea for six, Nellie started home, and she never once looked at the people who stopped and stared at her. At home she went straight to the kitchen, put on her apron, and began to prepare dinner. Her back was to the door so she didn't see Terel enter.

Terel had been told by her friends that Nellie was a sight to behold, and so she'd rushed home to see for herself; but even forewarned, she was not prepared for her first sight of Nellie. She had never seen a woman more beautiful than Nellie. In all of Chandler only the twins, Houston and Blair, could hold a candle to Nellie. And the blue velvet dress emphasized her newly slim body.

Anger surged through Terel, anger at being betrayed by her own sister.

Terel put on a smile and walked forward. "Nellie, you look beautiful, really beautiful."

Nellie turned and forced a smile. "It's a lovely dress, isn't it?"

"Yes, really lovely, but do you think you should be wearing it in the kitchen? I know it is only money, but aren't you concerned with ruining such an expensive dress?"

"Yes, how thoughtless of me." Nellie removed her apron and started upstairs, Terel close behind her.

"I am so glad to see that you've lost weight. I guess I can say it now, but you don't know what an embarrassment you've always been to Father and me. There were times we hated to be seen with you. Not that we don't love you, but we love you in spite of the way you look, do you know what I mean?"

As Nellie stepped out of the velvet dress her stomach growled with hunger. "Yes, I think I know what you mean."

Terel scrutinized Nellie's figure in the borrowed corset. "It looks as if you're going to need all new clothes, so perhaps I'd better choose them for you. Maybe you didn't realize that velvet doesn't exactly fit with working in the kitchen. Or maybe now you don't want to cook for Father and me. Maybe now you'd rather go to one ball after another and dance with men like Mr. Montgomery. Maybe more men—"

"No!" Nellie half shouted. "No more men. I don't trust them. I want nothing to do with them. You choose the dresses, I don't care what I wear." She

pulled on her oldest housedress, which now hung off of her, and ran down the stairs, buttoning as she went.

Once in the kitchen she grabbed a pie, still hot from the oven, and began to eat it. "No more men," she said aloud. "No more men."

If Nellie wanted nothing to do with men, the same couldn't be said for men regarding her. After having been ignored by the male population all her life, suddenly she was besieged with invitations. Handsome young men waited for her outside her house, then followed her wherever she went. They offered to carry her purchases, run errands for her. They invited her everywhere.

There seemed to be nothing Nellie could do to discourage them. She didn't talk to them, didn't so much as smile at them. She made no physical effort to make herself more pleasing to them. She wore the drab, oversized dresses Terel chose for her; she never minded when Terel burned her hair with a curling iron. But nothing seemed to put the young men off, for the truth was, now nothing Terel did could hide Nellie's beauty, and Nellie's reserve only encouraged the young men.

At home Nellie listened to Terel, because once she hadn't listened to her and she'd been duped by a lying, traitorous man.

"You don't want to go to the Christmas party at the Masonic Lodge, do you?" Terel asked, looking at the invitation. "You remember what happened at the Harvest Ball, don't you? I don't think I could bear seeing my beloved sister make a fool of herself like that again."

"No, I don't want to go," Nellie whispered, feeling very hungry. After two months, just the thought of Jace still made pain shoot through her. "I don't want to embarrass you or Father."

"It's not that you embarrass *us,* it's that you embarrass yourself, what with eating so much all the time, and then, of course, you have no taste in men. I'd be afraid the town drunk would walk in the hall and you'd believe you were in love with him."

"Terel, please . . ." Nellie pleaded.

"Oh, I am sorry, Nellie, I didn't mean to hurt you. I guess I'm just overly protective, that's all. Here's an invitation for you to sing with a choir. You don't want to do that, do you? I mean, there will be men there, and you know how you are."

"No," Nellie said, tears beginning to choke her. She didn't want to go anywhere. She just plain wanted to disappear.

"I really do think it's for the best that you stay home, at least for a while. Are those cupcakes? They smell delicious. Why don't you have one or two? People are saying you're too thin." She kissed Nellie's cheek. "I'll see you this afternoon."

When Terel was gone, Nellie ate a dozen cupcakes.

Jace stepped off the train and breathed the cold Colorado mountain air. It felt good to be back, good to return to the place he'd come to think of as home. He gave a boy a nickel to carry his bag to the hotel and check him in. He didn't want to take the time to go to the hotel first. All he wanted now was to see Nellie.

He smiled as the cold, dry air hit his face, and he patted his breast pocket where all Nellie's letters lay, tied with a ribbon. It had been two and a half months since he'd seen her, the longest ten weeks of his life, but it had taken that long to arrange everything. When he'd first arrived in Warbrooke and found his father to be perfectly healthy, his impulse had been to jump right back on the train and go back to Chandler. He'd had no doubt the rotten Terel was behind the phony telegram.

But the telegram had made him realize how much his parents meant to him, so he'd gone out sailing, just he and his father, and he'd found himself telling his father all about Nellie. At the end of the day's sailing he'd known what he wanted to do with his life. For all that he loved the sea, for all that he knew he'd miss it, he knew he wanted to live in Colorado with Nellie.

That night he'd written her and told her of his plans. He didn't tell her that someone had created the telegram. He didn't want to fight Terel from across a continent, so he just wrote of his plans. He planned to remain in Warbrooke long enough to sell most of his holdings, the land and house he and Julie had owned, all three of his sailboats, and he needed to work out property divisions with his brothers and father. When that was done, he planned to return to Chandler and make her his wife.

He'd written her long letters telling her of his home

town, telling her about his father and brothers, telling her of his mother's music and how good it was to hear her sing again. Once he was in Warbrooke he realized how little he and Nellie had talked, so he found himself pouring out everything to her. He told of visiting the grave of Julie and his little son and how his grief for them had been merely a dull ache. He wrote of the future he had planned for them, and one night, very late, when he was feeling very lonely, he told her of the trick he'd pulled on her by taking her to the Everetts' house. And always, repeatedly, he told her he loved her.

Nellie's letters to him hadn't been as long as he would have liked; in fact, they were almost curt, but they had been enough to let him know that she was all right. He hadn't written to tell her he'd be arriving today because, unexpectedly, he'd found a buyer for his last sailboat, and he was at last free. He had thrown clothes in a bag and taken the next train out of Warbrooke. He wanted to spend this Christmas with Nellie, and next Christmas his family promised to come to Colorado to visit him and Nellie and—he grinned—maybe his first kid.

Now, leaving the train station, he was on top of the world. Everything was cleared away for him and Nellie. Nothing else stood in the way of their happiness.

He was so happy, so engrossed in his thoughts that he didn't see the way the people of Chandler stopped and stared at him. They stared, then they frowned, then they put their heads together and muttered about how he had dared to return to this town.

He was walking so rapidly, trying to get to Nellie as quickly as possible, that he didn't see the door to The Famous swing open and Terel's friends step out. He walked right into them and packages went flying.

"Excuse me," he said, stooping to pick up packages, "it was all my fault. I wasn't watching where I—"

"You!" Louisa said.

Jace looked up at the three young women and was puzzled to see them looking at him in horror.

"How could you dare show your face in the town?" Charlene said, teeth clenched. "After what you did to Nellie!"

"Is Nellie all right?" Jace asked, rising.

"As if you cared," Louisa hissed.

Mae had not said a word, but suddenly she whipped out her hand and slapped Jace across his cheek. "I will *not* have your child," she said, pushing past him. Louisa and Charlene, after snatching their packages from him, followed her.

Jace put his hand to his cheek and stared after the women. "What in the world is going on?" he said aloud.

After that encounter he slowed his pace and began to notice the unpleasant looks he was receiving from nearly everyone he passed. He was beginning to feel like the villain in a melodrama.

Three blocks from Nellie's house he saw Miss Emily.

"I wouldn't have thought you'd have the nerve to return," Miss Emily said. "I guess you heard that Nellie's, shall we say, dilemma was a false alarm, so perhaps you figured it was safe to return, but I doubt very much if Charles will give you the freight company now."

She started to walk past him, but he caught her arm. "Would you please tell me what's going on?"

Miss Emily looked down her hawklike nose at his hand on her arm, and Jace dropped his hand. "Is no woman safe from you?"

"Safe?"

Miss Emily started to walk away, and Jace's temper got the best of him.

"What the hell is going on?" he bellowed.

Miss Emily was disgusted by his language, and she was furious with him for hurting Nellie, but something in his tone made her halt and turn back. "Where have you been since the Harvest Ball?" she spat at him.

"Home in Warbrooke, Maine. I sold everything I owned there so I could come back and marry Nellie and live here in Chandler."

Miss Emily stood blinking at him. "Why didn't you tell Nellie?" she whispered.

Jace was sure everyone in this town was crazy. "Tell her? I've been writing to her since I left." He pulled the packet of letters from inside his coat pocket, pink and yellow silk ribbons dangling from them. "Here are her letters to me, and"—he pulled a little box from his trouser pocket and opened it to reveal a ring with a big yellow diamond set in gold—"this is the engagement ring I plan to give to Nellie. It's been in my family for years. Think she'll like it?"

Miss Emily was trying to recover herself. A man whose family had a ring like that probably didn't need a small business like Grayson Freight. "Oh, my goodness, what in the world is going on? Do you have engagement rings for the other young ladies of this town?"

Now Jace was sure the people were crazy. "No," he said patiently. He hadn't thought Miss Emily was senile, but he thought so now. "I only marry one woman at a time. Perhaps you have me confused with Bluebeard. Now, if you'll excuse me." He tipped his hat and turned away.

"Mr. Montgomery!" Miss Emily called, halting him. "You and I must talk."

"We'll talk later, I promise. Right now I want to see Nellie."

Miss Emily firmly clasped her arm to his. "You and I have to talk *first. Before* you see Nellie. I think there are some things you need to know." When he opened his mouth to protest, Miss Emily continued, "I'm not sure Nellie will see you."

"See me? But Nellie has agreed to marry me." He held up the letters.

"I don't believe Nellie wrote those letters. Nellie believes, as does the whole town, that you jilted her."

For a moment Jace couldn't speak. He glanced

down the street toward Nellie's house. "Perhaps we should talk," he said softly.

It was an hour later that Jace left Miss Emily's house, and he was in a rage, a towering, furious rage.

"You'll never guess who I saw today," Johnny Bowen said to Terel. He was walking her home from her shopping expedition, carrying her packages.

"Who?" Terel asked, not really caring. She knew that Johnny was just walking her home in hopes of getting a glimpse of Nellie. Since the Harvest Ball, and especially since Nellie had lost weight, it seemed that every man in Chandler wanted to court her. As Miss Emily had laughingly said one day, "Nellie has everything: beauty, brains, a sweet temper, a rich father, and she can cook. She is every man's dream." And it seemed as though Miss Emily was right, because men seemed to swarm around Nellie. Not that Nellie paid any attention to them, but the more she ignored them, the more they tried to get her attention. Terel could no longer go anywhere or have anyone to her house for all the questions about Nellie.

"I saw that man, Jace Montgomery."

Terel stopped in her tracks. "You saw him? When? Where?"

"Here in Chandler, about an hour ago. He and Miss Emily were talking. Actually, it looked almost as if they were having a quarrel, but I was across the street and couldn't hear what they were saying. He didn't look too happy."

Terel quite suddenly didn't feel very well; in fact, she felt quite frightened. She put her hand to her forehead and swooned against Johnny.

"Terel, are you all right?"

"I'm ill," she whispered. "Take me inside."

"Sure." He put his arm around her shoulders and started to help her walk.

"Carry me, you fool," she hissed.

"Oh, sure." Johnny bent and picked her up. "You're heavier than you look." Struggling, he got her up the stairs, across the porch to the front door, then had to balance her on one knee to open the door. He was sweating, and his back was straining. "On the sofa?" he asked, his voice high with effort.

"Upstairs, you idiot, and call Nellie."

Johnny leaned against the wall at the bottom of the stairwell and panted. "Nellie," he said, little more than a whisper.

"She'll never hear you if you don't speak up."

"Nellie!" Johnny yelled.

"Again."

"Nellie!" His voice lowered. "Terel, what did you eat for breakfast? Rocks?"

She heard Nellie coming. "Get me upstairs, and slowly."

"That's the only way I can move." Groaning, Johnny started up the stairs, his arms and back aching.

"Terel?" Nellie said. "Oh, Terel, what's wrong?"

"Nothing, just a little dizzy spell. It's probably just my heart."

196

"Put her in here." Nellie directed Johnny to Terel's bed. "Go get Dr. Westfield. Tell him to come at once. Tell him it's the utmost emergency!"

It was at that moment that the front door slammed open and the whole house jarred. *"Nellie!"* Jace Montgomery bellowed. "Where are you?"

All the blood drained from Nellie's face as she stood up straight.

"Nellie." Terel grabbed her sister's arm. "Oh, my dear Nellie, it's him, and I'm too sick to help you face him. I will do what I can to help you. Johnny, send him away."

Johnny looked horrified. "The man is twice as big as me."

Downstairs they could hear Jace going from room to room.

"I must go to him," Nellie said softly.

"No, don't leave me. Please, please, Nellie, don't leave me. You say you care for my comfort, so will you leave me when I might be dying?"

"No, no, of course not."

"Swear you won't leave me. Swear it."

"I will not leave you," Nellie whispered. "I do not believe I *can.*"

The three of them stood silently as they heard Jace thunder up the stairs, and then he was at the doorway. He was more handsome than Nellie remembered: bigger, more alive.

The anger on his face softened when he saw Nellie, and in spite of what she knew to be true about him, she stepped toward him, but Terel clamped down her hold on Nellie's arm. "Don't leave me," Terel whispered.

"What can I do for you, Mr. Montgomery?" Nellie managed at last to say.

"I've come to take you away, to marry you." After what Miss Emily had just told him, Jace wanted nothing more than to strangle Terel. He had no doubt she was behind all the gossip that had been spread about him. He was sure she was behind the letters he'd received and believed were from Nellie.

"I am perhaps a fool once, but not twice," Nellie said. Her heart was pounding.

Jace couldn't contain his anger. "As long as you stay around her you'll be a fool forever."

Terel tightened her grip on Nellie and gave a little whimper.

"My sister is ill, she—"

"Ill? She's sick, all right, sick in her mind." He tried to calm himself. "Nellie, I love you. I went home because I received a telegram saying my father was dying. I wrote you a note. I explained where I was going and why. I wrote you letters all the time I was gone."

"We received no letters, Mr. Montgomery," Terel said.

"You stay out of this," Jace said, glaring at her. "I don't know how you've done this, but I know you're behind it. For two cents I'd—"

"Do not speak to my sister like that. She is ill. Johnny, go get the doctor."

Since Mr. Montgomery was blocking the doorway, Johnny wasn't about to push past him. He stood where he was, pressed into the corner of the room.

"Look at this." Jace pulled the packet of letters from inside his coat and threw them on the bed. "I received these from you while I was in Maine." He looked at Terel. "What did you do with my letters to Nellie?"

Terel took the letters before Nellie could touch them. "Whose handwriting is this? It's not Nellie's, and it's certainly not mine." She tossed the letters to the floor at Jace's feet.

"You little—" Jace began, starting toward Terel.

Terel lifted herself from the pillows and hid behind Nellie. "He's going to kill me! Nellie, save me!"

"Mr. Montgomery, you have to go."

"I'm not leaving here until you let me explain."

Nellie was beginning to recover her equilibrium. "I think not. No, let me speak. You have had your say. I'm afraid, sir, that once I believed everything you said to me. I defied my family for you, but not again. I cannot give my trust to you twice. You broke it once, and I cannot trust you again."

"Nellie," Jace said, and the word came from his heart. "I never did anything to break your trust. I wrote to you, I—"

"I neither received nor sent any letters."

"That's because *she* took them."

Terel clung to Nellie and whimpered.

"My family loves me and would have no reason to

harm me. You, on the other hand, have wanted my father's business. You have even courted the old maid daughter hoping to get it."

Jace took a deep breath and tried to calm himself. "Nellie," he said softly, "your sister has every reason to want you to remain with her. You are little more than a slave to her. You cannot buy the kind of loyalty and maid service you give her. She has merely to wish for something and you give it to her."

He took a breath. "As for my wanting you just to get your father's freight office, don't you realize that my family owns Warbrooke Shipping? I could buy your father's company with my pocket change. Everyone else in town seems to know of my money." He squinted at Terel hiding behind Nellie. "I never wanted your money; I've only wanted *you.*"

Nellie's head whirled. Was what he said true? If she believed him about the letters and his wealth, she'd have to believe that her family had had a hand in lying to her. Her family loved her. They would never want to harm her. They wanted her happiness.

"Nellie, come with me," Jace said softly, holding out his hand to her. "I've loved you from the moment I saw you. Please come with me."

She wanted to go with him. God help her, maybe she was a silly, desperate, love-starved old maid. Maybe he had lied to her. Maybe if she went with him he'd seduce her, get her with child, then abandon her, but at the moment she didn't care. She wanted to take his hand, walk out with him and never look back.

But she couldn't. She *could not* leave her family. As

though chains held her, she felt she could not leave them and make them so—well, uncomfortable. Who would cook for them? Look after them? See to their needs?

"I cannot," she whispered.

Jace dropped his hand, and the pain showing on his face was raw. "You won't."

"I cannot."

Jace looked at Terel. "It looks like you win. My love isn't as strong as your selfishness." He looked back at Nellie. "I'll be at the Chandler House for three days. Come to me there." He turned and left the room.

The three left behind listened until the front door shut. Johnny peeled himself away from the wall and looked at Nellie. "You should have gone with him," he said softly, then he left.

I know, thought Nellie, but she couldn't explain to anyone how she felt. *She could not leave.*

Terel settled back against the pillows. "I'm glad that's over. Nellie, I think I'd like some tea, and perhaps a slice of the cake you made this morning."

Nellie turned to look at her sister. Was there any truth in what Jace had said? Had he written her, and had Terel destroyed the letters?

"Nellie, don't look at me like that. You're giving me goose bumps."

Was she nothing more than a slave to her family? "Did you know he was wealthy?" Nellie whispered. "Is it true? Is he?"

"If he were wealthy, would he have taken a job as a clerk for Father? Would he have paid court to a woman no one else in town would have? Sometimes, Nellie, it's shocking the way you seem to believe strangers over your own family. Why, for a minute I thought you were going to go with him. Going to leave the people who love you for a man you don't even know." She caught Nellie's hand. "You wouldn't leave me, would you? You promised you wouldn't."

"No, I don't believe I can." She pulled away from Terel. "I'll get your tea now."

"And don't eat the whole cake. Father would like some, too."

Nellie stopped in the doorway, and the look she gave Terel was icy. "I do not believe my weight is any longer a cause for concern. If you haven't noticed, *you* are the plumper sister now." Nellie turned away and went down the stairs.

Chapter Ten

THE KITCHEN

*B*erni left the Food room, and immediately she was again wearing her burial suit. She had been eating for quite some time, eating all the delicious things she'd denied herself on earth in order to stay slim, but now she was standing in the hall and thinking.

Pauline appeared out of the fog. "Have you been to the Fantasy room yet?"

Berni's eyes widened. "What kind of fantasy?"

"Anything you want."

Berni perked up. "Medieval men? Dragons?"

"Anything." Pauline stepped toward a golden arch, Berni behind her, but Berni halted.

"I was wondering what happened to Nellie. Did she lose the weight? Did she marry her hunk?"

"She lost the weight, but she doesn't see Mr. Montgomery anymore. He's still in Chandler, but I think he's about to give up hope. Nellie won't see him. Right through here is the Fantasy room."

"Wait a minute. Why doesn't she see Montgomery? I thought he'd like her when she lost the weight."

"Mr. Montgomery loves her—his love has nothing to do with her size—but Nellie is bound by the wishes you gave her. She can't leave her father's house and disturb the comfort of her father and sister."

"Oh," Berni said, looking down at her feet. "I never meant to do her harm. She seemed like a nice kid. I thought—"

"What does a fatty like Nellie matter anyway?"

"Nellie matters. Look at the way she was always helping people. People like that count. Nellie never—"

She stopped because Pauline had stepped through the Fantasy arch and the fog had cleared. Before them was indeed a scene out of Berni's wildest dreams. A beautiful young woman with blonde hair to her waist, wearing a clinging pink silk gown, was chained to a post. Before her was a large but rather cute dragon, with a forked tongue and fire coming out of his nostrils, fighting an incredibly handsome, muscular, dark-haired man wearing chain mail. Berni nearly swooned.

"Come on," Pauline said, "you can be the maiden."

Berni took two steps forward, then stopped. "No, I want to see about Nellie."

"Nellie can wait. Did you see the man's horse?"

The fog cleared to the right, and there was a beautiful black stallion draped in red silk.

Berni swallowed and took a step backward. "No," she tried to say firmly, but her voice quavered. "I want to see Nellie."

Abruptly, fog closed over the scene, and Berni let out a sigh of relief. She grinned at Pauline. "Anyway, I'd never be able to choose between the man and the dragon."

"Your choice," Pauline said, and she led the way through the fog to the arch of the Viewing Room.

Berni settled down on the banquette and watched as the fog before her cleared and she saw the Grayson living room. Nellie was there putting branches of pine along the mantelpiece.

"She looks great," Berni said. "She's really built, and now she's much prettier than her little sister, so what's the problem? Why doesn't she have Montgomery? In fact, why isn't she at some party? Looking like that, she could have *any* man."

"Nellie has never been much interested in appearances. All she's ever wanted was to love and be loved. Mr. Montgomery sensed that."

Berni watched Nellie hanging up Christmas decorations, tying greenery along the banister. She was so very pretty now, but in her face was a deep, deep sadness. When Berni had first seen her, and Nellie had been fat, Nellie hadn't looked sad as she did now. Berni couldn't understand it. On earth she'd spent many thousands of dollars for plastic surgery so she could look half as good as Nellie, yet here Nellie was, with a face that could cause a war, a body better than any centerfold, and she was all alone and looking miserable.

"So why doesn't she go after him?" Berni snapped.

"Two reasons: because of the wish you gave her and because Nellie doesn't know how. You can't just put wolf's clothing on a sheep and expect the sheep to turn into a wolf. Nellie is Nellie, whether she's fat or thin."

Berni turned away from the scene, putting her hand to the side of her eyes. "I can't bear to see any more."

Pauline waved her hand, and Nellie and the room disappeared.

"So now what happens?" Berni asked.

"That's up to you. We supply the—"

"Yeah, yeah, I know. I'm supposed to supply the wisdom. I haven't been exactly wise so far, have I?"

"Oh, well, what does one fatty more or less matter?"

Berni winced. "You've made your point. So maybe I was wrong. You said Montgomery loved her. Would she be with him now if she wasn't bound by the wish?"

"Probably, but who knows? One can't predict these things."

Berni looked back at the fog. "I would like to know more about Nellie. Is it possible to see all of her life? From the beginning?"

"Of course." Pauline waved her hand, and there was

a pretty woman in a Victorian bed straining to give birth.

"I'll leave you," Pauline said, rising. "I'll return when it's nearer Christmas 1896."

Berni waved her hand absently and stretched out to watch. She'd already learned that time in the Kitchen wasn't like earth time. The scenes seemed to fly past. Berni saw that from the beginning Nellie was a quiet, solemn, eager-to-please child. Her mother wasn't well, so Nellie was never allowed to make even the smallest sound; and since her father's business made little money in its early days, Nellie always had many chores. As a reward for all her obedience, Nellie was pretty much ignored by her parents.

When Nellie was eight her mother gave birth to Terel, then was seriously ill until she died four years later. But Nellie didn't mind caring for the child. She held the screaming infant and looked at it with love. For the first time ever she was going to have someone who would return her love.

After his wife died, Charles Grayson seemed to have no qualms about leaving his twelve-year-old daughter with the responsibility of caring for the baby. Nellie was a good mother, but she was so starved for affection that she gave the baby anything she wanted, so that Terel grew up believing that Nellie had been put on earth solely to do Terel's bidding.

In adolescence Nellie began to gain weight. Berni saw the way boys flirted with Nellie, making her blush, and how she looked back at them. Then, at home, Charles would forbid Nellie to go out and leave the toddler alone. Nellie would go to the kitchen and eat.

By the time Berni got to 1896, she really understood Nellie's life. Nellie had no idea how to fight for what she wanted. All she knew was how to give.

Berni watched as Jace Montgomery came into Nellie's life, saw the way she blossomed under his love, and Berni smiled warmly. Nellie deserved to have someone love her, deserved to stop being a slave to her father and sister.

Things changed when Nellie started giving her three wishes away, and Berni felt herself grow smaller. She hadn't meant to hurt Nellie. Heaven help her, Nellie had had enough pain in her life, and she didn't need any more, but the wishes had increased Nellie's burdens.

Berni watched Nellie at the Harvest Ball and thought she looked beautiful. A little wide, perhaps, but she was so in love her entire body glowed. After the ball Berni saw what Terel did with Jace, sending the phony telegram, then stealing Jace's letters to Nellie and hiring some poor woman to write replies to him so he'd think Nellie had answered him.

"You conniving little manipulator," Berni muttered.

She watched as Jace returned to town, then saw the scene when Terel pretended to be ill. Berni heard Jace ask Nellie to leave with him, and she heard Nellie say she *could not* leave. "Because of the third wish," Berni said aloud.

At last she came to Nellie hanging the greenery in

the parlor. It was two days since Jace had asked her to leave with him and three days before Christmas.

The scene became covered with fog.

"What shall it be?" Pauline asked. "More wishes?"

"Can I go back to earth and help Nellie?"

"Go back to earth? You want to leave the Kitchen? Leave here for all the nastiness of earth? You know, you didn't see all of the Feasting room. They have chocolate mountains in there. And it's not wimpy milk chocolate but that really deep, rich, dark chocolate. You can eat all you want and never gain an ounce."

Berni hesitated as she imagined chocolate mountains. "No," she said firmly, "I want to return to earth. Nellie needs a teacher. She's no match for that sister of hers. She needs some help."

"But I thought you liked Terel. I believe you said she reminded you of yourself."

"Terel is *exactly* like me, and that's why *I* need to fight her."

"Fight her?" Pauline said. "But I thought you wanted to make her into Cinderella."

"She already thinks she *is* Cinderella. What right does she have to take everything away from Nellie? Nellie is a hundred times the person she is. Can I go to earth or not?"

"You may go, but the limit is three days, and I warn you, these visits rarely work out."

"I'll take my chances. Now, I'll need to know some about the family. I plan to arrive as the Grayson family's long-lost relative, their very rich relative. Do you think I might have a wardrobe, something in green silk to match my eyes?"

Pauline smiled. "I think something might be arranged. There are rules, though. What has happened stands. You cannot change what Nellie has already wished."

"I don't plan to disturb her family's comfort," Berni said with a smile. "They'll be the most comfortable family in America."

"And three days," Pauline said. "That's all the time you have."

"I won my second husband in three days, and I didn't resort to magic. How about a hat with an ostrich plume? And how about shoes with lots of buttons?"

"I hope you do this well," Pauline said softly.

"I always get what I want. Terel doesn't stand a chance against me."

Pauline sighed. "All right, then, come along. We'll embed you in the memory of the Graysons so they have some knowledge of Aunt Berni, then we'll send you down."

"And clothes," Berni said. "Don't forget clothes. How about an amber necklace?"

"You will have all the clothes you want. I hope I don't regret this—and, more importantly, that Nellie doesn't regret this."

"Don't worry. When it comes to being a bitch, I wrote the book."

"That's a book I don't want to read," Pauline muttered as she started walking.

CHANDLER, COLORADO
1896

"How rich?" Terel asked, biting into one of Nellie's crispy apple tarts.

"*Very* wealthy," Charles said, putting down the letter. "And she has no other relatives besides us. It's my belief that she wants to choose one of you as her heiress."

"*One* of us?" Terel asked, glancing sideways at Nellie, who was sitting at the far end of the dining table. As usual, Nellie wasn't paying attention. Not that Nellie was ever a barrel of laughs, but in the last two days, since that man had come storming into the house, Nellie had been a veritable gloom factory. "Why just one of us?"

"She says she doesn't want her fortune divided. She wants it kept intact after her death, so I take that to mean she plans to leave it all to just one of you."

"Mmm," Terel said thoughtfully. "I do wish you'd told us of her visit before the day of her arrival."

"I can't think why I didn't," Charles said, genuinely puzzled. "I'm sure I knew about the visit, but I don't know why I never said anything."

"Oh, well," Terel said, licking her fingers, "I shall do my best to take care of her. Nellie, you had best stay in the kitchen and cook. Your wonderful cooking will please Aunt Berni, I'm sure."

Nellie didn't bother to reply. She pushed the food about on her plate. For once in her life she wasn't hungry. Being hungry meant that you were alive, and right now Nellie didn't feel very alive.

Terel turned to Nellie and studied her. Yes, it would be much better to keep Nellie away from this rich relative. Terel wouldn't have worried about the fat Nellie engendering love, but this new Nellie, slim, beautiful, unconsciously graceful, caused people to look at her twice. For the life of her Terel couldn't figure out what about Nellie caused people to care so much about her. Miss Emily, the nosy old hag, constantly asked after Nellie, as did whole churches full of people. Terel assumed it had to do with the way Nellie kept giving their food away to the grubby kids of Chandler. No one ever thought to thank their father for paying for the food, nor did they thank Terel for having to do without because Nellie spent their family's money on other people. No, everyone just saw Nellie playing Lady Bountiful.

Now Nellie looked like the heroine of a tragic play, with her big eyes full of misery. Everyone who saw her seemed to be filled with pity for her. But why? Terel wondered. She'd come close to marrying a very rich man—not that Nellie deserved him—and in the end, she'd done the right thing by staying with her family, so why was she trying to make everyone else feel miserable? Terel knew Nellie's moroseness was meant to punish her, Terel, but no one else seemed to realize that. That stupid Mae Sullivan said yesterday that she felt almost like telling Nellie the truth about Mr. Montgomery, that he hadn't kissed any other woman in Chandler. "Except me," Terel had said, and she turned on her heel and walked away.

Why were people such fools? Terel wondered. Why couldn't they see that Nellie was so much better off with her family? Who knew what this man Montgomery was like? Maybe he was abusive to women. Maybe he drank. Maybe he was an impostor and not really rich at all. Maybe Terel had saved Nellie from a fate worse than death.

Anyway, Terel thought, forget about the man; there was Aunt Berni to think about. Terel thought she would make an excellent heiress. Paris, Rome, San Francisco, she thought. Furs, jewels, houses.

She looked again at Nellie. She'd better keep this rich aunt away from Nellie, in case she was one of those do-gooders who would fall for Nellie's sad face. Terel didn't mean to lose a fortune just because Nellie was temporarily a little upset.

"I think I'll make up some menus," Terel said thoughtfully. "We mustn't skimp while Aunt Berni is here." She smiled at Nellie, thinking of the complicated dishes she'd order. Nellie wouldn't get out of the kitchen for a week, and as Aunt Berni's visit was only going to be for three days . . .

Nellie was in the kitchen when she heard the commotion of her aunt arriving. She didn't go out to greet her because both her father and Terel were there. She heard her father's voice raised and the sound of men grunting as they carried trunks up the stairs. After a half hour or so Nellie prepared a tray with a mug of hot cider and a plate of Christmas cookies to take to her aunt. Just as she was leaving the kitchen Terel burst in.

"She brought six trunks of clothes with her," Terel said, partly in horror, partly in admiration. "And she's fifty if she's a day, but she doesn't have a line in her face."

"That's lovely for her."

"Perhaps." Terel picked up a cookie and munched it thoughtfully. "There's something about her that I don't trust. There's something in her eyes."

"Maybe she's lonely. Didn't Father say she lived alone?"

"It's not loneliness, I can assure you of that. There's something I don't understand in her eyes."

Nellie pushed open the kitchen door. "I'll just take her some food and say hello."

Berni sat in the parlor and smoothed her velvet skirt. She liked these ornate Victorian clothes: no synthetic fibers, lots of hand embroidery, intricate detailing. What she didn't like was Terel. It hadn't taken Berni but moments to see that Terel was out to get what she could for herself. Berni looked at her and smiled and thought, I'll get you, brat, and I won't need to resort to magic.

When Nellie entered the room Berni's face softened, for she recognized the goodness in Nellie. All the images Berni had seen of Nellie's childhood flashed before her eyes, and before she thought she gave Nellie a radiant smile.

Terel, just behind Nellie, saw that smile, and she vowed to find out what it meant, but she betrayed no wariness as she offered her Aunt Berni cookies and cider from the tray Nellie held. An hour later Terel was able to slip away from the house and find the dreadful child who called himself Duke.

"Well?" Terel demanded of the boy. He wouldn't speak until she'd put a quarter in his hand. "Have you been watching the hotel like I told you to?"

"Sure thing, and this mornin' there was a message in Montgomery's box. I didn't see nobody put it in there, it was just *there.*"

"Did you get it?" she snapped impatiently.

He handed her the note, and she read it quickly. It was an invitation to luncheon today at the Grayson house, and it was signed by Nellie. But Terel knew the note hadn't been written by Nellie; the way it was worded wasn't the way Nellie would write. She crumpled the note in her hand. It had to have been written by this Aunt Berni, but how had she found out about Nellie and the Montgomery man?

"She's just like all the others," Terel muttered. "They all think of Nellie, and no one thinks of me."

"What's that?" the boy asked.

"None of your business. Now go back and continue watching."

The boy snorted and then walked away, hands in his pockets, whistling.

As Terel started back to the house she began to plan. She didn't know why this Aunt Berni was here or what she wanted, but Terel meant to find out.

When Terel returned her Aunt Berni was in the guest bedroom, lounging on the bed eating chocolates and reading one of Terel's novels. "There you are, my dear," Berni said. "I was hoping you'd return soon. You will help me unpack, won't you?"

"Nellie will—" Terel began, then she smiled radiantly. Better to keep those two apart. "I would be delighted to help."

Two hours later Terel was furious, but she managed to hide it. She hadn't "helped" Berni; she had done all the work of struggling with the trunks, opening them so they formed short closets, then inspecting everything to make sure nothing was damaged. The sight of the dresses alone was enough to make Terel vow to do anything to make Aunt Berni leave everything to her, but the jewels nearly undid her. "What is this?" she asked, holding up a long tube of what looked to be green glass.

"Actually, it's a magic wand. One long emerald," Berni said.

Terel gave a little smile, further angered that Berni would make fun of her. There's something wrong here, Terel thought again.

Luncheon came and went, and Berni was puzzled as to why Jace didn't come. He had seemed to genuinely like Nellie. So why didn't he accept Nellie's invitation? Perhaps a note wasn't strong enough; perhaps Jace needed to see Nellie in person.

After luncheon Berni suggested Terel take a nap. "You have worked so hard today helping me. You deserve a little rest."

"I do feel tired," Terel said, yawning. "I think I will take a nap." She went upstairs, climbed into bed fully clothed, and pulled the spread over her, concealing that she still wore her day clothes. Ten minutes later she heard the door softly open, and she saw Berni peek in at her and then silently close the door again.

Berni went downstairs to the kitchen, where Nellie was already working on dinner, and sat down on the other side of the big table. "You and I haven't had much time to talk, have we?"

"No," Nellie said, trying to smile, but she didn't feel much like smiling.

Berni once again felt guilt. It was her fault Nellie was stuck in the kitchen now. If Berni hadn't interfered, Nellie would probably be on her honeymoon right now.

"Nellie, if you could have one wish in the world, what would it be?"

Jace, Nellie instantly thought, but she stamped down the idea. "I guess I'd want my family to be happy."

"You mean, to get what they deserve in life?"

"Oh, no!" Nellie said, then she realized how that must sound. "I mean, yes, I want them to get what they deserve because they deserve only good things, but I wouldn't want them to be unhappy."

"All right," Berni said, "it's a deal. They'll get what they deserve, and they'll be happy with it."

For the first time in a long while Nellie gave a genuine smile. "You're very kindhearted, aren't you?"

Berni looked away. No one had ever called her kind before. She turned back to Nellie. "I have a favor to ask of you. I have some friends whose son is visiting Chandler. Perhaps you've heard of my friend, LaReina, the opera star."

"Yes, certainly I have, though I haven't heard her sing."

"Divine, utterly divine. Anyway, her son is visiting Chandler, and I'd like to ask him to dinner tonight, if that's all right with you."

"Of course you may invite him."

"But I was wondering if perhaps you would ask him. I think he may be a little shy."

"I would be glad to ask him. Where's he staying?"

"At the Chandler House. Just ask for Jace Montgomery. He—Nellie! Are you all right?" Berni hurried to the other side of the table and helped Nellie to a chair. "Did I say something wrong? Would you rather not have anyone here for dinner?"

"It's not that, it's . . . it's that Mr. Montgomery and I . . ."

"Oh, so you know each other, do you? That's wonderful." She helped Nellie to stand, then took her heavy wool shawl and her wool felt hat from a peg by the door. Berni jammed the hat on Nellie's head, wrapped the shawl about her, and shoved her toward the door. "Go and ask him to dinner. Terel is sleeping, so she's comfortable, and your father isn't here. Everyone is taken care of, so you're free to go."

"I can't ask him," Nellie whispered.

"For me? For your dear old aunt?" Berni said pleadingly.

Nellie took a deep breath. Her heart was pounding. "All right. For you." She stepped out the door into the cold, snowy air and started walking toward the hotel.

Berni shut the door and smiled. Easy, she thought. Almost too easy. Jace probably hadn't come to lunch because he hadn't received the note, but Berni knew Nellie was a person who took her responsibilities seriously and would no doubt sit down and wait for Jace to give him the message personally.

She sat down at the table, started munching Nellie's cookies, then snapped her fingers and the 1989 Christmas issue of *Vogue* appeared in her hands. This fairy godmother stuff is a cinch, she thought. She'd probably have Jace and Nellie together by ten o'clock tonight. Maybe they'll name their first kid after me, she thought, smiling.

On the other side of the kitchen door Terel tightened her mouth into a firm line. So that's it, she thought. Their aunt was a friend of the Montgomery man's mother. *That's* why Aunt Berni had so suddenly and unexpectedly come to Chandler. It had nothing to do with choosing one of the Grayson girls to inherit. Aunt Berni wanted her friend's son to marry Nellie.

And leave me behind, Terel thought. Nellie gets to marry a rich man and get out of this dreadful town while I have to stay behind.

Tiptoeing, Terel made her way across the room and out the front door without making a sound. "Nellie!" she called, once outside.

Slowly, Nellie turned to her sister. "I thought you were taking a nap."

"I was, but I was afraid to leave you alone with her."

"With Aunt Berni?"

"Yes, with her. I tell you, Nellie, my every instinct cries out to beware of her."

"But she seems so nice. I don't think—"

"You didn't think there was anything wrong with that awful man who said he loved you, either."

Nellie looked down at her hands.

"Where were you going?" Terel asked.

"To the . . . ah, Aunt Berni asked me . . ."

"She didn't ask you to see *him,* did she? Oh, Nellie, she is cruel. This is unspeakable! How could she do something like this to her own flesh and blood?"

"I don't think she meant any harm. She merely wanted me to ask her friend's son to dinner."

"And you think that was mere coincidence? You think she just 'happened' to ask *you* to go to this man? You think she doesn't know every sordid detail of what's happened to you?"

"I didn't really think about it. She asked me to go, and—"

"And you obeyed her. Oh, Nellie, why don't you ever stand up for yourself? Tell her you're not going to degrade yourself more than you already have. Tell her the *truth* about the man."

"The truth?"

"Yes, that he made free with you then went off and left you, and that he walked out, and more, with nearly every female in town, and that he's a liar, saying he wrote you letters while he was away. Oh, Nellie, the man is a scoundrel. He's proven that repeatedly, but here you are chasing after him like you did the night of the Harvest Ball."

Nellie wrung her hands. She knew Terel was saying these things because she worried about her, but the words made Nellie feel really awful.

"All right, Nellie, I wasn't going to tell you," Terel said with a sigh, "but your Mr. Montgomery has been taking Mae out for the last two days." She put her hand on Nellie's arm. "I'm so sorry about him. I know you believed you cared for him, but you'll get over him. He's not worth shedding one tear over. Now that you've lost weight you're quite presentable-looking, so we'll be able to find you a husband. Ted Nelson needs a wife, and he's a very dependable man."

Ted Nelson was at least fifteen years older than Nellie. He ran a livery stable on the edge of town with his two big half-grown sons, who everyone said were so dumb that the horses were teaching the boys to read and write. It was debated around town whether any of the Nelsons had ever had a bath.

"Well, don't turn up your nose," Terel snapped. "Everyone says Ted Nelson has a fortune hidden somewhere. But if you don't like him, we'll find you someone else. Maybe we can look in Denver. No one there knows of your reputation. Maybe—"

"I won't ask him," Nellie said, putting her hands over her ears. "I won't ask Mr. Montgomery to dinner. Please stop."

"All right," Terel said tightly. "I don't know why I bother. Sometimes you act as though *I* am the villain." She slipped her arm through Nellie's. "Let's go to the bakery and get something to eat. You really are getting too thin."

At the moment Nellie felt hungry enough to eat the bakery itself—boardwalk, shingles, sign, and all.

Berni was again puzzled when, at dinner, Jace Montgomery didn't show up. She sat through the long, boring meal eating Nellie's delicious food and listening to Terel chatter. She watched Charles Grayson smile at his younger daughter and now and then frown at Nellie.

As far as Berni could see, losing weight had had no effect on Nellie's life. Charles and Terel had always treated her as someone to do their dirty work, and they didn't seem to think that her losing weight was any reason to change their attitude. Nor had the weight loss changed Nellie. Even though she was now a knockout, she still had very little self-confidence. Nellie wasn't encouraging the young men who came to call on her; she wasn't now demanding that her family treat her with respect. She was the same Nellie she had always been.

Berni winced when she thought of this Nellie. Poor substitute for a fairy godmother I am, Berni thought.

Maybe I should have done the "Bibbidi Bobbidi Boo" bit and changed a few pumpkins into coaches. Nellie got to go to the ball with her handsome prince, but only because someone else came up with a dress. Everything her fairy godmother had done for her had backfired.

After dinner Berni excused herself to her room. There she took a clear glass dome from the top of a lamp and put it on the table. "It's not a great crystal ball, but it's the best I can do," she said aloud. "Now, let's see what's going on."

She moved her hands over the globe, just as she'd seen countless gypsies do in the movies, and to her delight images began to appear. It took a moment for the images to appear clearly, but then she saw Terel talking to the big kid, Duke. She saw the note Berni had sent to Jace's mailbox, saw Terel take it, read it, and crumple it. She saw Terel talking to Nellie when Nellie was on her way to visit Jace at his hotel.

Berni leaned back in her chair, and at first her only thought was admiration. Terel was more clever by far than Berni had believed. Somehow she'd known Berni was out to help Nellie, and she'd managed to anticipate what Berni was going to do and then thwart her.

"If this keeps up, in two more days Nellie will be even worse off."

Berni looked at the fading images in the globe. She'd very much like to beat Terel without using magic, she thought. It would be a challenge to outfox this young woman, but the truth was she didn't have time. She had only three days in which to perform miracles for Nellie, and now one of those days was gone.

So, Berni thought, the first day was a draw. Let's see what can be done with the remaining two. First she needed a plan.

She tried wiggling her nose like Samantha on "Bewitched," but that didn't work, so she wiggled her ears instead. (In all her life on earth no one had ever known Berni could wiggle her ears.)

A chalkboard appeared before her, and a piece of chalk, hovering nearby, was ready to write. Berni leaned back in her chair.

Number one, she thought, and the chalk began to write, Nellie believes Jace left her, and that he fooled around with other women. Number two, she doesn't believe Jace sent her any letters.

And number three, Jace's feelings are hurt because he doesn't think Nellie returns his love. "And heaven help any woman who hurts a man's feelings. He'll go off and brood for a few hundred years or so." The chalk hesitated, then wrote "feelings hurt" very darkly. Obviously, the magic chalk was male.

"All right now, what else do we have?" She thought the names Terel and Charles, so the chalk wrote them in columns. Under them it wrote "can't disturb their comfort."

"Ah, yes, but they can get what they deserve if they're happy with it. Charles wants a clean house, good food, and to spend as little money as possible." The chalk wrote this under Charles's name. "Terel wants someone to take care of her, to give her everything before she knows she wants it."

When this was written Berni looked at the board. The obvious thing would be to show Nellie how little her sister and father cared for her, but Berni remembered the pain of hearing her own father saying he thought Berni was useless. "She never thinks of anything except clothes and how much money someone can give her," Berni had overheard her father saying. No, she didn't want to give that kind of hurt to anyone, and especially not to Nellie.

"So what can I do?" Berni whispered.

She leaned back in her chair, waved her wand, and began to look for the letters Jace had sent. It was so fascinating looking into people's houses, seeing some very odd things going on, that she almost forgot her purpose. But she at last found the letters, tucked away in a drawer in some poor woman's house. It was obvious Terel had paid her to answer Jace's letters.

Berni waved her wand again, and then, smiling at her own cleverness, she gave the letters to a crazy old woman and imbedded in her memory a complicated story of how she'd come by them. The old woman lived with her brother and his young daughter, and it looked as though the child could benefit from a fairy godmother of her own.

"You bring the letters to Nellie, and if I know her, she'll take care of you," Berni said.

She smiled and looked at the other problems outlined. Now all she had to do was get Jace and Nellie together someplace romantic.

It was nearly dawn when Berni at last had her plan mapped out. One thing good about being dead, she thought, was that she didn't need any sleep. She stood and stretched, wiggled her ears, and the chalkboard disappeared. Her plan was made and set into action now. She just had to stand back and see what happened.

Chapter Eleven

Nellie was awakened by someone throwing gravel at her window. She opened her eyes to see the early gray light of dawn, then got out of bed to go to the window. A young woman, hardly more than a girl, stood below, shivering in the early morning cold. She opened the window.

"Are you Nellie Grayson?"

"Yes," Nellie said. "Could I help you?"

"I have to talk to you. Could you come down?"

Puzzled, Nellie wrapped a heavy shawl about her nightdress, slipped her feet into slippers, hurried downstairs, then opened the kitchen door to the girl. "I'll have the stove going in a few minutes, and I'll make some coffee."

"No, please, I don't have time."

Nellie gave her a little encouraging smile as the girl stared at her. "You wanted to talk to me?"

"Oh, yeah. I just wanted to see you, that's all. I mean, I wanted to see what you looked like. On account of the letters."

"What letters?"

"These." The girl pulled a fat bundle of letters from under her shawl and handed them to Nellie. They were all from Jace, addressed to Nellie.

"Where did you get these?" Nellie whispered.

"I live way out of town—don't matter where, it's just my pa and me and his daffy old sister, my Aunt Izzy. See, my pa don't want nobody to know his sister's crazy, so he pretends she's not. Of course, pretendin' don't make her right in the head, but he pretends just the same. Anyway, one of the things my pa lets Aunt Izzy do is collect the mail when we come to town. I don't know how she done it the first time—probably just lied, 'cause she's a real good liar—but she told the postmaster's stupid kid that she was Nellie Grayson, so the kid gave Aunt Izzy your letters. I think she even told him they were secret, so he hid them from his pa and saved them for Aunt Izzy. Anyway, she got 'em all. If I hadn't cleaned her room yesterday, nobody ever would've known. I wanted Pa to bring me in last night so I could give you your letters, but he wanted me to burn 'em. I lied to him and told him I had, but this mornin' I set out first thing and brung 'em to you. I didn't wanta wake up the whole house, but I waked up that maid of yours first, and she told me which room was yours."

Nellie listened to the story, held the letters, and looked at them. Slowly, she was beginning to realize that Jace *had* written her. He hadn't abandoned her, but he'd written to her all the time he was gone.

"Them letters is important, ain't they?" the girl said softly.

"Yes." Nellie fumbled for a chair and sat. "The letters are very important."

The girl smiled. "I thought so. Well, I gotta go now." She started toward the door.

"Wait! Have you eaten? What will your father do when he finds out you've defied him?"

The girl shrugged. "Knock me around some. Nothin' much. He ain't real mean like some."

Nellie swallowed. "What's your name?"

"Tildy, for Matilda."

"Tildy, how'd you like to come to this house and work?"

"In this pretty house?" Her eyes widened.

"Yes, and I can assure you that no one will 'knock you around.' "

Tildy could only nod as her throat closed in happiness.

"Then come first thing the day after Christmas, and I'll have"—Nellie swallowed—"I'll have spoken to my father by then."

The girl nodded, her eyes still wide, and backed out the door. "Thank you," she managed to whisper before Nellie shut the door.

Nellie was heedless of the cold room; she forgot all about making food for her family. She opened the letters and began to read. It was all there, all of Jace's love, and a daily account of how he was selling everything he owned in order to come to her in Colorado. He talked of their future together. He told her of his family. She read about his mother's singing, about his father working so hard running Warbrooke Shipping. He wrote of his brothers and his Taggert relatives in Maine. In one letter he sent her a tiny sketch of an Australian orchid done by his Aunt Gemma. He wrote of his Grandpa Jeff and the old mountain men living in California and promised to take her there on their honeymoon.

By the fourth letter Nellie was crying. By the last letter she was crying so hard she didn't at first see Mae Sullivan standing over her.

"Mae," Nellie said, startled, "I didn't hear your knock."

"The door was standing open."

"That's odd. I'm sure I closed it." Nellie was trying to dry her eyes on the sleeve of her nightgown, pretending she wasn't actually crying at all.

"Oh, Nellie," Mae said, and she began to cry, too. "I couldn't sleep all night long. I don't think I'll ever be able to sleep again until I tell you the truth."

Nellie sat in stunned silence as Mae poured out the whole story, saying that every female in town was half in love with Mr. Montgomery, and half out of jealousy, half out of anger, they had told Nellie that he had tried to kiss them.

"It just didn't seem fair," Mae wailed. "He never even *looked* at any other woman in town. You hooked him before we even got a *chance* at him. And then, too, you were so fat we all thought he must be crazy for wanting you, so we figured he wanted your father's business and was courting you to get it. We just couldn't believe he really *liked* you. Oh Nellie, I am so sorry for what we said. Mr. Montgomery never even looked at another woman in this town except you."

Nellie clutched the letters and gaped at Mae. All she could think of was the awful, awful wrong she had done Jace.

"I'd better go," Mae said, sniffing. "I hope everything turns out all right for you. I hope you marry him and live happily ever after." She turned quickly and left the house.

Nellie sat where she was. Now what did she do? Jace was leaving today.

Before she could form another thought Berni entered the kitchen. "I thought I heard someone up." She looked at Nellie's letters. "Has something happened? Anything you want to talk about?"

"I . . . no," Nellie said. She wasn't used to talking about her problems to anyone. "I must get breakfast ready."

"In your nightgown?"

"Oh, no. I must change." She was having difficulty thinking clearly.

"Nellie," Berni said, "talk to me."

The next moment Nellie was seated at the table and pouring out everything to Berni. "I misjudged him. He was always kind to me, yet I believed the worst of him. How could I have hurt him so much?"

"Everyone hurts the people they love. What you have to do is go to him and tell him everything."

"I couldn't."

"It's not humiliating to tell the man you love that you love him. Half of love is groveling. You must—"

"I would do anything, say anything to get him back, but I can't leave the house. I must prepare breakfast, and my father is having investors to dinner tonight. I must—"

"Keep them comfortable, right?" Berni snapped.

"Yes, I guess so. It doesn't make sense, but I can't leave them."

"They'll sleep as long as you're gone."

"Sleep? But Father never sleeps past seven."

"He will today. Trust me."

Nellie looked at her aunt and knew she was telling the truth. "I will go to him."

"Good girl. Now go get dressed and wear the blue velvet."

Nellie started to ask how Berni knew of the blue velvet, but she didn't want to take the time. She wanted to see Jace as soon as possible.

Alone in the kitchen Berni snapped her fingers and was out of her nightgown and into a lovely dress of rust-colored silk broadcloth. The lace at her neck was handmade. She sat down at the table, snapped her fingers again, and a month's supply of *People* magazine appeared, along with a plate of croissants and a pot of mocha. Now all she had to do was wait. Once Jace saw Nellie he'd forgive her everything, and wedding bells would soon be ringing. She just had a little bit more to do with Charles and Terel and then she'd be done. She might at last get to try the Fantasy room in the Kitchen. But instead of dragons, how about cowboys? Maybe he'd be a scout and she'd be a spunky young lady who needs to rescue her father or brother, and the scout won't take her because she's a woman, but then . . . Well, anyway, she'd have to try it when she returned.

With a shaking hand Nellie knocked on the door of Jace's hotel room. Her heart was in her throat as she planned what she'd say to him.

He opened the door, his face full of sadness, but when he looked at her the sadness left and was replaced with anger. "Come to say goodbye?" he asked, then he walked away from her. He was packing.

"I came to apologize," she said, stepping into the room. "You were right about everything. I was totally wrong."

"Oh?" he said, putting shirts into his case. "Wrong about anything specific?"

"This morning a girl brought your letters to me. It seems her aunt lied to the postmaster's son, and the letters were given to the aunt rather than being delivered to me."

"How interesting," he said, but there was no interest in his voice.

"And this morning Mae came to tell me that she and her friends had lied. You didn't try to . . . to kiss them."

"No, I didn't," he said, turning for a moment to glare at her.

Nellie took a breath. "I came to apologize for all I said and even for what I thought."

He walked toward her, and Nellie's heart almost stopped, but he just kept walking toward the bureau to get his razor. "So now what am I supposed to do? Say that everything is fine? Forgive you for everything and start all over again?"

"I don't know," she said softly. "I only know that I love you."

He paused for a moment, his hands on the clothes in his case. "I've loved you, too, Nellie. I've loved you from the first day, but I'm not strong enough to fight your family. You believe everything they tell you. I don't want to spend my life fighting for a piece of you."

"I didn't know," she said. "I didn't know about the letters."

He turned to look at her. "And you didn't know about Warbrooke Shipping either, did you? Tell me, did your father put you up to coming here? Or did you make a pledge with your greedy little sister? If you get Warbrooke Shipping you'll give them— What? A hundred dresses a year for Terel, new freight wagons for your father?"

Aunt Berni had said to grovel if she must, but Nellie couldn't bear any more of this. "My family has only wanted what's best for me. They did not want me to marry a man who left town without leaving a message, or one who courted many women at once. There was no proof that you had sent letters or that you hadn't—"

"Kissed all the girls?" he said angrily. "There *was* proof. There was *my* word. You should have believed me. You should—"

"Yes, I should have," Nellie said, fighting tears. "But I didn't. I'm not much of a fighter, Mr. Montgomery. I just wanted to do what was right for everyone concerned, and it looks as though I've failed. I apologize for inconveniencing you."

"Your apology is accepted," he said tightly. "Now, if you don't mind, I have a train to catch."

There was a knot rising in Nellie's throat, a knot that threatened to choke her. She couldn't speak. She just nodded then and left the room, walking down the stairs and out of the hotel. She walked home, but she wasn't aware of moving. As surely as though she'd been killed, she knew her life was over.

Berni sat in the kitchen, still reading *People* magazines, when she heard the front door open. She expected Nellie, her handsome hero on her arm, to come running into the kitchen. Instead, Berni heard Nellie's heavy footsteps going up the stairs.

"Now what?" she mumbled. "Antony and Cleopatra didn't have this much trouble." She snapped the magazines and mocha and chocolates away and went upstairs. Nellie was prostrate on the bed. She looked about two inches away from suicide.

"So tell me," Berni said, licking her fingers.

Nellie didn't answer, so Berni wiggled her ears.

"He says I should have believed him," Nellie whispered.

"Ah, men like blind obedience. Nellie, let me give you a little advice from somebody who's known a few men. I don't know if you've heard this or not, but there's a saying that man's best friend is a dog and that diamonds are a girl's best friend. Man's best friend is a dog because that's what he wants a woman to be: a dog. He wants a pretty little wife, preferably blonde, who will do whatever he wants, when he wants it. He wants to be able to say, 'Come on, let's go,' and she'll get up, tail a-waggin', and follow him. He doesn't want her to ask questions about where or when or how, and he does *not* want her to have an *opinion.*

"For a woman, she's found out that she can trust something like diamonds because they don't run around at night, nor do they constantly point out how she *should* behave."

These words seemed to have no effect on Nellie, so Berni continued. "Don't you understand? You weren't his best friend."

"I have other responsibilities."

"Yes, of course you do, but you're trying to talk logic to a man who's in love. Being in love is enough of an alien emotion to a man; you can't try to introduce logic to him, too." Berni looked down at Nellie, who was softly crying into her pillow, and knew she was making no sense to her. The first time a woman fell in love she was so full of hope, so full of the belief that if she could just get this guy then everything in her whole life was going to be fixed, that never again would she be angry or lonely or would her skin break out. Love was going to solve every problem. Berni knew it was no use trying to tell Nellie a few truths. Truth had nothing to do with love.

"All right," Berni said, sighing. "I'm sorry things didn't work out. Maybe it's best to forget him."

"I'll never be able to forget him. He has been so good to me, and I have treated him very badly. Now he hates me, and I deserve it."

Berni wanted to tell Nellie about sex, wanted to tell her to use her beauty and sexiness to capture Jace, but she knew Nellie would never understand. Nellie had no idea how to go about *taking* what she wanted.

This morning, after she'd sent Nellie off to see Jace, she'd thought her job was over, but she'd underestimated how hurt Jace was. It was time for Plan Two. She closed her eyes and did a little wishing and rearranging of people.

"Nellie, what you need is to get your mind off this man. Reverend Thomas stopped by and asked you to run an errand for him."

"I can't," Nellie said into the pillow. "I have to see to my family."

"Oh, your father and Terel have already left the house."

Nellie turned to look at Berni. "Left? But they have guests coming today. I have to prepare the food."

"Not today. They'll be gone all day, so you're free."

Nellie sniffed. It wasn't like her family to leave unexpectedly. "Where did they go?"

"To Denver. Your father received a telegram saying

his investors wanted to meet with him in Denver today, so he went up there. And Terel went with him."

"Terel went with Father to a business meeting?"

"Hard to believe, isn't it? But that's what she said, that she wanted to help her father with his clients. Between you and me, I think this had something to do with it." From behind her back Berni pulled a Denver newspaper. "Look on page six."

Nellie sniffed and sat up, took the newspaper, and opened it. " 'Christmas Eve special,' " she read. " 'Every clothing item in every store in Denver is on half-price sale today only.' " She looked at Berni. *"Every* store?"

"All of them, so I guess that makes you free for the day. How about going to see Mr. Montgomery again?"

The tears started anew. "I couldn't. He . . . he doesn't want anything to do with me."

Berni sighed. "Unfortunately, you're probably right. So maybe you ought to spend the day doing whatever the preacher wants you to do."

"I don't think I feel up to seeing anyone. I think I'd just like to stay in my room today."

"Of course. I understand. Broken hearts take a long time to mend. Besides, those kids don't need anybody. They'll be fine. Maybe after Christmas someone else can tend to them." She stood. "I'll go and leave you alone."

"What children?"

"What do you mean, what children?"

"The children you said don't need anybody."

"Oh, them. Nobody special, just a few orphan kids.

That good-looking preacher said they were alone out at someplace called . . . now, what was it? Journey?"

"Journada? That falling-down old ghost town?"

"That's it. He said the kids were out there alone and hungry, but it doesn't matter. They'll find food, or maybe they won't. It's not your problem. Why don't you stay in bed, and I'll bring you up a tray? I'm quite handy in the kitchen. I—"

"The children are alone? With no food?"

"That's what he said. How about some nice hot chocolate? Or maybe—"

"I'm going to them," Nellie said, getting off the bed.

"I don't think you should. After all, they're just a bunch of kids. Who cares if they starve or not?"

"*I* care. Do you know where they are in Journada?"

"In one of the shacks. Nellie, you can't go out there all alone."

"I *must*. The children can't be left alone. I guess Father took the buggy, so I'll have to rent one."

Berni sighed, trying to hide a smile. "If you are determined to go, then you could borrow my carriage."

"You wouldn't mind?"

"No, of course not. I'll prepare a food basket while you go to the stables and get it."

As soon as Nellie was out of the house Berni got her emerald magic wand from her trunk and waved it over the bed. A large basket appeared. "Now, what to eat?" she murmured, then she waved her wand and a couple of Cornish hens, wrapped in bacon and stuffed with bread crumbs and preserved fruit, appeared.

She had a great time conjuring up food, then bottles of wine. She added a damask table cloth, Limoges china, and heavy silverware. Leaning back in her chair, sipping on brandy-laced coffee, she directed everything into the basket. Of course it wouldn't all fit, so she had to put a little spell on the basket, then a second spell when she realized the basket weighed over a hundred pounds.

"They'll never notice," Berni said. "Lovers always think everything is magic. A bell rings and they think it's because of them. A small basket produces an endless quantity of food and no doubt they'll take it in stride."

She directed the basket to float down the stairs ahead of her and only just grabbed it as Nellie entered the room. Nellie had the buggy waiting, ready to go off to save the hungry children.

"Good luck," Berni called after her as Nellie took off. Berni went back to the parlor, pulled her magic wand out of her pocket, and waved it. The end of the parlor disappeared, and she could see the train depot. Jace Montgomery was standing before the ticket window.

"I'm sorry, sir," the ticket agent was saying, "but you've missed the train."

"Missed it? I'm fifteen minutes early."

The agent looked at the clock on the wall behind him, then at his pocket watch. "That's true." He frowned. "I don't think the train's ever been early before. Late, yes, but never early."

"When's the next train?" Jace snapped.

"It's . . ." The agent trailed off as he looked at the schedule. "That's odd. Usually there's a train through here every thirty minutes, but today there isn't another train for four hours." He looked at Jace and shrugged. "Maybe it's because it's Christmas Eve."

"Some Christmas!" Jace muttered. He grabbed his case and started back to the hotel. What he wanted to do was get drunk, so drunk he wouldn't remember ever having been to Chandler, Colorado.

Berni waved her wand and Jace disappeared. Another wave and she saw Terel in a Denver store fighting a tough-looking woman for a silk blouse. The store clerks looked ready to drop from exhaustion as they tried to wait on the hundreds of pushing women.

"I may have overdone it on the sales," Berni said, but she waved her wand so she saw the Denver street. "Now, Terel dear, who can we find for you? Someone you deserve, but someone who will make you happy." She scanned the street until she saw an old buckboard. In the back were six kids, three of whom were rolling about trying to kill one another. On the seat in front was a big, dirty, but good-looking, farmer who ignored the kids.

"Well, well, well, just who are you?" She reached into the air to retrieve a computer printout. "John Tyler," she read. "Thirty-two years old, widower with six illiterate, loud kids. Raises pigs. Very poor, will always be poor. Good heart. Vigorous in bed."

Berni looked back at the man as he got down from the wagon seat. "Not bad. Not bad at all." She looked at the kids. They were a handsome bunch, even if they were as dirty as the pigs they raised. "Just what Terel needs: someone to think of besides herself. A few years of cooking and cleaning and washing should teach her a little humility."

She waved her wand and the picture split down the middle, Terel on one side, John Tyler on the other.

"Okay, kids," Berni said, popping a chocolate into her mouth. "Meet and fall in love. Don't just fall in love; fall madly, passionately in love *forever*. Got it?"

She waved her wand and Terel dropped the blouse she was looking at and started for the front door of the store, while John Tyler turned away from the feed store and headed toward Terel. "Terel Tyler," Berni murmured. "It could be worse."

She waved her wand again, and this time she meant to take care of Charles. He had always been so penny-pinching, so afraid to spend any money, that he'd forced his eldest daughter practically into slavery.

Berni watched Charles at his meeting, watched him eyeing what the businessmen were ordering for lunch. She could see he was dreading the bill. "What he needs is someone to help him spend his money."

For Charles Berni found a pretty widow in her forties, a woman who believed talk of money was impolite conversation and who had no idea there was any connection between her many expensive dresses and the fact that her husband had died and left her penniless.

"Fall in love, Charles," Berni said, and she waved her wand.

"That takes care of them. Now let's see about Nellie." She waved her wand and saw Nellie just as she was arriving in the old town of Journada. She still had to search the buildings for the kids, so Berni knew she had time.

Berni waved her wand over herself and was suddenly wearing a black velvet walking suit, a saucy little hat perched over her left eye. As she reached the front door of the Grayson house she snapped her fingers and it began to rain and thunder, the wind blowing fiercely.

Berni stepped outside and got a face full of water. "This is ridiculous," she muttered, then she snapped her fingers and the area over her stopped raining. In perfect dryness she walked to the hotel. Around her people were struggling so hard against the rain and wind that they didn't notice Berni walking in a dry, calm place. A few people, looking out windows, saw Berni walking in a dry spot, but they rubbed their eyes and didn't believe what they saw.

Berni arrived at the Chandler House just as Jace was downing his sixth whiskey. "Are you Jocelyn Montgomery?" Berni asked, looking down at him seated at the table. They were the only people in the bar at this hour of the day.

Even two thirds drunk as he was, he winced at the name. "Jace," he said.

"Your mother told me Jocelyn."

He looked up at her. "You know my mother?"

"Quite well. When I told her I was coming here to visit relatives she asked me to say hello to you. I meant to yesterday, but I . . . I . . ." Berni started crying so she could no longer talk.

Jace was instantly on his feet as he helped her to sit down. "I'm sorry, ma'am. Can I be of any help?"

"I'm just so worried," Berni said, sobbing into a lovely linen handkerchief. "It's my niece. She went out into this storm to deliver some food to orphaned children and hasn't returned yet. I'm so worried about her."

"I'll get the sheriff for you, and he can send some men out to look for her. Do you know where she went?"

"A place called Journada. She's lost, and it's all my fault! There are no children out there. The children are at the Coronado Mine. I got the names mixed up. My Spanish never was too good."

Jace patted her shoulder, and she could smell the whiskey on his breath. Actually, it wasn't a bad smell at all. She'd had some interesting times with men who smelled like he did. She looked at him over her handkerchief. Too bad she had only a day and a half left; too bad she was trying to be on her best behavior. Jace Montgomery was a *very* sexy man.

"The sheriff will find her. I'll go get him now." He started out of the room. "Oh," he said at the doorway, "what's your niece's name?"

"Nellie Grayson."

Jace just stood there blinking for a moment. "Nellie is out there alone in this storm?" His voice was rising. "You sent *Nellie* out to a broken-down old ghost town?"

"It was an accident. I just got the names mixed up. Spanish was—" She didn't say anymore because Jace was gone.

Berni leaned back in her chair, took Jace's glass of whiskey, and drained it. She propped her feet on another chair, then pulled her wand from her little purse (the wand was conveniently collapsible) and waved it. Before her appeared Jace tearing into the stables, throwing a saddle over an enormous black stallion (Berni sighed at the sight of the animal, a proper horse for a hero), and galloping away. Berni split the screen and watched Nellie searching through the shacks in Journada.

It wasn't long before Jace was there, and Berni sighed in anticipation of the coming romantic scene. But the scene didn't happen. The two of them stood under a leaky porch.

"What the hell are you doing here?" Jace shouted at her.

"I came to give food to hungry children," Nellie shouted back.

"There aren't any kids here. Your daffy aunt got the towns mixed up. You have to come back to Chandler with me. Your aunt's worried about you."

He turned away as though he expected Nellie to follow, but he looked back and frowned when she remained where she was. "I told you that you have to return."

"No," Nellie said. "I'm not going."

"What?"

"I'm not going anywhere with you."

Jace (and Berni, watching) gasped. *"Now* she stands up for herself," Berni muttered in disbelief.

"You can't stay here in this storm. These shacks are about to fall down."

"What does it matter to you?" Nellie yelled at him. "I am nothing to you."

Jace was across the porch in seconds, his face furious as he grabbed her shoulders. "You could have been everything to me, but you chose your family over me."

"I am not a dog, Mr. Montgomery, to follow you blindly. I love my family, and of course I'd believe them over you. Wouldn't you believe your family over a stranger?"

"I'm not a stranger. I'm—" He broke off.

"You're what?"

"Nothing," he said, and he dropped his hands and took a step backward. "You have to return with me."

"I most certainly do not. I am an adult. I got out here by myself, and I can return without your help."

"I guess you can at that," Jace said, his face hard. "Good day, Miss Grayson. Perhaps we'll meet again." He turned and started to walk away.

"Freeze!" Berni shouted, and the picture did freeze, Nellie at one end of the porch and Jace at the other, his back to her. "I have never seen two more hard-headed people in my life," she muttered. "I know the course of true love is never supposed to be smooth, but this is ridiculous. Now let me think."

She looked at the two of them under the porch, the rain pelting down, then smiled. "What are the sexiest words in a romance novel?" She deepened her voice. " 'We'd better get you out of those wet things. It looks like we're gonna be here all night.' "

Berni grinned, then snapped her fingers. A huge bowl of butter-dripping popcorn appeared. She leaned back in her chair. "Go to it, kids. You're on your own. If you can't handle it by yourselves from here on, you don't *deserve* a happy ending."

Chapter Twelve

*J*ace turned back at Nellie's scream. The end of the porch where she'd been standing was gone. It had collapsed under the weight of the rain, and Nellie was nowhere to be seen. He covered the distance to the end of the porch in two strides and saw Nellie floundering about in a deep pool of water. He didn't think about what he did but jumped in after her.

"Nellie, are you all right?"

"Yes," she yelled back, gulping water and clinging to him.

The pool was deep but not very big, so he was able to pull her to the side in just a few strokes. He grabbed her waist and, finding a toehold, pushed her up to the safety of the muddy street.

"Let's get out of here," he shouted when he was out

of the pool. Rain was beating him in the face. He put his arm around her protectively, and they began to run to the old stables where her buggy and his horse were tied. But just as they reached the building a brilliant flash of lightning lit the sky and thunder cracked over their heads. Jace's horse reared, Nellie's horse reared, and both horses broke away from where they were tied. Jace pulled Nellie to him as the two horses ran past them into the rain.

Jace stood for a moment staring after the horses. He knew he had not only tied his horse but shut and bolted the stable door. The door hadn't looked rotten enough that the horse could have broken it so easily.

A shiver from Nellie made him turn his attention to her. With his arm still around her he led her down the street to a dilapidated old house that was falling in on one side, but he could see a chimney, and he hoped the fireplace was still working.

There was firewood stacked inside the house, and after checking to see that the flue was clear he built a fire, blowing on a little pile of dried sticks and paper. It was some time before he had the fire going and he turned to look at Nellie. He knew he was wet and cold, but Nellie's lips were blue.

"Do you have anything else to put on?" he asked. "Is there something in the buggy?"

"I . . . I don't know," Nellie said, teeth chattering. "It's Aunt Berni's buggy."

"I'll go see." He went outside into the rain, ran to the half-rotted stables, and searched the carriage. He found a small lap robe and the picnic basket. Bending over to protect them from the rain, he ran back to the house. Nellie was shivering even harder. He knelt and threw more wood on the fire, then opened the basket and withdrew the tablecloth.

"It doesn't look like there's a chance of this rain letting up, and I can't find the horses until morning." He looked up at her. "Maybe you'd better get out of those wet clothes. You can wrap this around you."

Silently Nellie took the tablecloth and walked to the far side of the room. Her hands were so cold she had trouble unfastening the buttons of her dress. She kept glancing at him, at his broad back as he knelt before the fire. She didn't understand why she'd been so angry at him earlier, but she hated his insinuation that she was interested in him for his money. The *last* thing she cared about was his money. If she had realized that he loved her, she would have lived with him in the worst hovel in America.

When she was down to her chemise and knickers she hesitated to remove them, but they were cold and clammy next to her skin. She looked at Jace and her hands began to tremble even more, but this time not from the cold. With shaking fingers she removed all of her clothing and wrapped the tablecloth about her bare body. She unpinned her hair and shook the wet mass about her shoulders.

She walked back to the fire and stopped a little behind Jace. "You look cold, too," she said softly.

"I'm all right," he answered, and there was hostility in his voice.

What was it Aunt Berni had said about men, Nellie

wondered. It hadn't made sense at the time, but now she remembered something about Jace not thinking she was his best friend. He was right: She hadn't been his friend.

She sat on the floor very near him. "How is your brother's foot?"

"All right," Jace said tersely, not looking at her.

"And did your mother get over her cold? Is she singing again?"

"Yeah." He snapped out the word. "Everybody at home is fine." He turned to glare at her. "And they'll be glad to see me again. People at home trust me. They don't believe I'm a liar."

She couldn't bear his stare. She looked back at the fire. "I was wrong," she whispered. "I told you that. I tried to believe you, but I couldn't believe you'd want someone like me." She looked back at him. "I *still* can't believe it. You could have any woman on earth. Why would you want an old maid like me? I'm not exciting, I quit school when I was fourteen, I'm not anything special at all."

"You make me feel good," he said softly, and he leaned toward her as though he might kiss her, but then he pulled away. "You did make me feel good. I thought you felt about me as I did about you, but I was wrong. I think you believed you loved me in spite of the fact that I was a low-life, philandering nobody who was after your father's money."

"True," she said. "I did. After the Harvest Ball, after I heard so many dreadful things about you, I still went to my father's office to see you. Even thinking the worst about you I still loved you. It has been a joy to discover that I'm in love with a good man."

For a moment he seemed to sway toward her, then he pulled back. "A rich one, you mean. Tell me, has your father drawn up any contracts having to do with Warbrooke Shipping? Is that why you lost weight? Did you and your family think you could snare a rich fish easier with a skinny worm?"

"How dare you," Nellie said under her breath. "I never even knew about your money until after you'd returned from abandoning me."

"I didn't abandon you!" He stood and glared down at her. "I received a telegram saying my father was very ill. I suspect your treacherous little sister sent it."

Nellie also came to her feet. "You leave my sister out of this. Terel has been a great comfort to me. All those months you were gone and no word from you, I—"

"I wrote you. I wrote you about everything. I sold every stick of furniture, every blade of grass I owned so I could come be with you, and then you told me to get out of your house."

"And you told me I had three days, yet when I came to you, you threw me out," she shouted back at him. "Maybe one of your other women would have left her family in three days, but I couldn't. I would have followed you anywhere."

"Ha! You can't leave your dear sister for even one day. You may as well be a prisoner in their house. You cook for them, clean for them, adore them. And for what? What do they give you in return? They don't want you to marry and leave them, because where else could they find such a servant as you?"

His words were too close to home. She turned away as tears started to form.

He took a step toward her but didn't touch her. The tablecloth had fallen off her shoulders, and he could see them shaking with her tears. "Nellie, I'm sorry," he said softly. "It hurt more than I can say to find out that my love wasn't returned. Maybe I've been spoiled, I don't know. I've only fallen in love once before in my life, with Julie, and she loved me in return. There was never any question that we loved each other. Julie trusted me, she——"

"And her family knew your family?"

"Of course. We'd grown up together."

"My family didn't know you. You were a stranger to us and you . . . you paid attention to a woman no man in town had ever even looked at, much less loved. You——"

"That is the strangest damn thing," Jace said, his voice rising. "What's *wrong* with this town? I was glad the men saved you for me, but they must all be blind or stupid. You're by far the prettiest girl in town, you're smart, you're funny, and you're the most desirable female I've seen in years."

Nellie turned to look at him. "You're the one who's blind. I'm fat old Nellie Grayson, only good for cooking and ironing and——"

He pulled her into his arms and kissed her. "You were made to love and be loved. Why couldn't they see that?"

"I'm glad they didn't," she whispered against his lips. "If I'd married someone else, I wouldn't have met you."

He held her against him, and his hands roamed over her body until Nellie wasn't sure she could breathe. He released her abruptly. "Look—ah—this is going to be a long night. Maybe we ought to eat something and get a little sleep."

Nellie looked at him and knew what she wanted to do. She wanted him to make love to her. Maybe out of her own stupidity she'd lost her only chance for marriage and a home of her own, but she wasn't going to lose this opportunity to spend the night with the man she loved. She wasn't going to let pride or convention stand in the way of one night with this beloved man.

She smiled at him and moved the basket nearer to the fire. As she looked inside it she said, as though it meant nothing, "You'll catch your death in those wet clothes. You'd better remove them. You can wrap up in the lap robe." He didn't say anything and she didn't look at him, but she heard him turn and walk to the far end of the room.

Nellie was shaking as she withdrew one package of food after another from the basket. She couldn't identify some of the items. In the bottom were three bottles of wine, one of champagne, plus lovely crystal glasses. She was wondering how the glasses had not been broken when she saw Jace's bare foot across from her.

She looked up slowly, up muscular calves to heavy thighs, then a small robe about his waist. She'd never seen a nude man before, and the sight of Jace's broad, thick, sculpted chest made her mouth dry.

She sat back on the floor with a thunk. "Oh my," she whispered. "My goodness, my."

To his consternation, Jace found himself blushing. "I, ah, ah . . . anything good to eat in there?"

Nellie kept looking at him and swallowing. She had no idea an unclothed man could be so utterly, splendidly beautiful.

"Champagne," he said, bending to pick up the bottle. He quickly popped the cork, then, sitting, he filled two glasses and reached across the basket to hand Nellie one. "What shall we drink to?" he asked.

"To love," she whispered, her eyes roaming over his body.

"Oh, God, Nellie," he said with a groan, then he quickly pushed the basket out of the way and was on her. "I can't wait for our wedding night. I've wanted you since the first time I saw you." He was kissing her neck. "I've behaved so well. I've kept my hands off you, but I can't bear this torture any longer. Please," he whispered.

"Teach me," she whispered as she kissed his ear. "Teach me everything."

He didn't answer as he kissed her neck, his hand

moving the cloth off her shoulder. When he had the
cloth half off her body she could feel his skin against
hers, his hairy roughness against her soft smoothness.
His body was so lean and hard, so full of planes and
angles. She ran her hand down the side of him. His lap
robe was gone, and she touched the leanness of his
buttock.

"Nellie," he whispered before his mouth descended
to her breast.

There were no words or thoughts to express how his
mouth felt. That this man who had taught her so
much, who had given her the greatest gift of all, love,
should give her this wonderful, heavenly, physical joy
was almost more than she could bear.

Instinctively she arched her body up against his as
his tongue made circles on her breast. His hand ran
down her body, caressing her, touching her skin. He
moved his hand inside her thighs, stroking, kneading,
making her feel things she never dreamed existed.

He rolled to the other side of her, his body slightly
off of hers. Nellie looked at him in the firelight, his
eyes half closed with desire. His lips were full and
slightly parted. She touched his lips, running her
fingertips over them lightly, then ran her fingers down
his neck, across his chest, down his hips and to his
thighs as far as she could reach.

She closed her eyes and put her arms around him,
and he moved fully on top of her. Nellie wasn't sure
what she was doing, but instinct, desire, and love
combined to make her raise her hips to him.

When he first entered her she gasped at the pain, but when he started to withdraw she clasped him to her. "Don't leave me," she whispered.

"Never."

He went slowly with her, pausing now and then, waiting while she adjusted to this new emotion. "Nellie, I . . .", he said, and then he was blinded with passion. Nellie's eyes opened. He hurt her, true, but this building force in him, this overpowering, all-consuming passion she felt in him touched some inner, deep woman's core of her, and she lifted her hips higher to receive him.

With his final thrust she wrapped her legs about him and pulled him deeper and closer to her. She wanted all of him that she could get.

Jace lay on her for a moment, his body lightly covered with sweat. "Did I hurt you?"

"No," she said, only half lying.

"Nellie, I meant to wait. I meant to wait for a bed and a beautiful hotel suite and—"

She put her fingertips to his lips. "I am more than happy. If I never have any more than this, it will be enough. I will always remember this night. When I am home alone I—"

"Alone?" He lifted off of her. "Home? What is this, blackmail? You mean you're *still* choosing them over me?"

"I thought you were going back to Maine. Just this morning you were packing."

It took a moment but he relaxed against her, moving to the side and pulling her close in his embrace. "I figure I would have made it to Chicago before I turned around and came back. I'm not sure I could make it without you. My entire family—aunts, uncles, cousins, all of them—laughed at me for being so lovesick while I was home. All I wanted was to get back to you."

She snuggled her cheek against the bare skin of his chest. "I ate. I was so miserable while you were gone that I ate pounds of food. Whole cakes. Pies. One day I ate an entire rump roast."

He ran his hand down her body, over her flat stomach, down her slim thighs, and frowned. "What happened to you? Half of you is gone."

"Not quite half. I don't know, I just kept getting thinner by the day. Don't you like my new size?"

"I guess I'll get used to it, but if you wanted to gain some weight I wouldn't mind."

She smiled at him. "Every other man thought I was fat before. They—"

"Fat? You looked great. Not that you don't look great now, but . . . Nellie, I love you no matter what size you are. Just so long as you aren't one of those women who picks at her food. I can't stand that. Women should laugh and eat and sing and enjoy life." He smiled down at her. "They should be like you were at the Everetts with all those kids."

"Tell me about the women you know who laugh and eat and sing."

He pulled her to him and told her about growing up in an old, enormous house in Maine and it being filled with happy, energetic women who came to sing with his mother. He remembered long meals with so much food on the table the center would bow, and the women would eat for hours and tell stories of who was sleeping with whom, and they'd sing. They'd argue about how an aria was to be sung. Jace's father, 'Ring, would sit at the head of the table and be the judge. He'd make the women sing the arias again and again and again, then he'd tell the women they were each perfection. The women always pretended to be offended, but they loved having a handsome man as their adoring audience.

"And were you also an adoring audience?"

"I loved every one of them. I loved their voices, their tempers, their demands. I loved their big breasts and big hips. I loved the enthusiasm they had for life. They ate, drank, loved, and raged with passion."

"I'm not sure I am as . . . as passionate as those women."

"You love your family so much you were ready to give *me* up for them."

She knew he didn't realize how vain he sounded. "That was no great sacrifice. You were a penniless clerk in my father's office."

"I took the job to be near you. I never wanted to imprison myself, but a man in love will do a lot of foolish things."

She snuggled his arm across her chest. "You came back for me. I did doubt you, and I'm sorry. I won't doubt again."

"Now you'll go with me?"

"I'll follow you anywhere. I'll be as faithful as a . . . as a dog."

He laughed at that. "What if your little sister tells you I've kidnapped the Sunday School class?"

"I might believe the choir, but not the Sunday School."

He squeezed her tightly. "Nellie, answer me. It's my whole life you're playing with."

Part of Nellie was fearful. Lately there had been something compelling about her family, something so compelling that she felt she *couldn't* leave. Not as long as her family needed her.

"Nellie," Jace said, as though warning her.

"Terel needs me." She could feel him getting angry. "Maybe we could find her a husband. How many brothers do you have?"

He relaxed at her joke. "Not enough for your little sister. She could—"

Nellie turned in his arms and kissed him. "The fire's going out, and I'm hungry. Maybe we could eat, and maybe we could do this again. Is that possible?"

He bit her earlobe. "I might be able to manage it." He rolled away from her, then watched her pull the cloth back over her body. "You really don't mind having our wedding night early?"

"There will be a wedding?" she asked softly.

"As soon as I can arrange it. That is, if you agree—and, considering the hell you've put me through, you damned well ought to agree."

"Yes," she said, her heart in her eyes. "Yes, I will

marry you and live with you and bear your children and love you forever."

He kissed her hand. "That's all I want of you: your body, soul, mind. I want every part of you."

"What do I get in return?"

"All my love. Contrary to popular opinion in this town, I love only one woman at a time."

"As faithful as a diamond?" she asked, eyes twinkling.

He smiled, then, stretching, reached for his wet coat. He looked in the inside pocket and withdrew a box. "Speaking of diamonds . . ." He opened the box to show her the ring with the big yellow diamond. "For you," he said softly. "If you'll have me. Me and my temper and my jealousy."

"I'll have you with or without the ring, with or without money." She looked at him, love in her eyes. "I really don't care about your money. It's you I love."

"I know that. Give me your hand."

He slipped the ring on her finger and kissed her gently. "Now, about that wedding night," he said, pushing her to the floor.

They made love, then ate hugely, then made love again, then ate again. Toward dawn they slept, wrapped about each other's bodies, tired but happy.

A strong, bright ray of sunshine came through a broken window and woke Nellie. She sat up with a jolt.

Jace, still half asleep, reached for her to pull her back down to him.

"I have to go," Nellie said, trying to pull the tablecloth from under Jace so she could cover herself, but he was too big to budge.

"Nellie," he said, his tone tempting her back into his arms.

She rolled away from him and went to the corner where her clothes were heaped. They were still damp and cold, but she struggled into them as quickly as she could.

Jace rolled onto his stomach and looked up at her. "Honeymoon over?"

She paused a moment as she looked at him, all six feet of him stretched out, bronze skin against white damask, and almost dropped her clothes and ran to him. She caught herself. "I have to get back. My family will be worried about me."

"Worried about their breakfast, more likely," Jace muttered, but not so Nellie could hear. Something she'd said last night had made him pause. She'd asked if he wouldn't have believed a Montgomery over a stranger. Whatever else Nellie's father and sister were, they were her family, and it was only right that she believe them.

"I'll find the horses," Jace said, and reluctantly he stood and began to dress. "Think there's any food left in here?" he asked as he opened the basket. There was so much food left it looked as though they'd not touched it. "This thing is bottomless."

"It seems that way," Nellie said, looking over his shoulder. He caught her to him. "Maybe it's just me, but everything seems to be more beautiful than it's ever been in my life."

"I agree," he said, kissing her.

Nellie was the first to push away. "I have to return."

Jace sighed and released her. *"If* I can find the horses."

At that moment an answering nicker came from outside, and he opened the door to see both horses standing in the mud as though they were waiting to return. "My luck has run out," Jace said heavily, making Nellie giggle.

Within minutes he had her buggy hitched and his horse tied behind. As soon as they stepped into the buggy their euphoric mood left them. They didn't talk. Both of them were afraid of what awaited them at the Grayson house in Chandler.

Berni greeted them at the door. At first she was concerned about their long faces, afraid they hadn't made up their differences. (Berni had stopped watching them after they'd entered the cabin and had, instead, used her wand to spy on her former twentieth-century friends.) But then she saw their fingers entwined and realized that their sad faces were from dread of Terel and Charles.

"At last!" Berni said. "Nellie, the most incredible thing has happened!"

"Are Terel and Father all right?" Nellie asked dully, clasping Jace's fingers.

"More than all right. Look at this telegram from your father."

Nellie read it twice before she looked up. "Terel has eloped?"

"It seems she fell in love with some farmer and married him the same night. She doesn't even want to come back for her clothes; she wants them shipped. And your father is marrying someone, too. He wants to stay in Denver until the wedding."

Nellie just stood there blinking.

"You're free, Nellie, free," Berni said.

Jace frowned. "You know, there's something odd going on here. Yesterday there was that pool of water Nellie fell in, and then this morning it was gone. And the horses ran away even though I'd locked them inside the stables. And there was that bottomless basket of food. And now this. I think—"

Berni narrowed her eyes at him. "Haven't you ever heard the old saying 'Don't look a gift horse in the mouth'? Nellie is free of her obligations to her family and free to marry you. Are you questioning that?"

"No, I just . . ." He stopped and smiled. "You're right. I'm not questioning anything. Well, Nellie, how about marrying me next week?"

"Yes," Nellie said softly, just beginning to realize that she was indeed free. "Oh, yes, I'll marry you." She turned to Berni. "You'll stay for my wedding, won't you?"

"I can't. My job's done now, and I have a date." She smiled. "A date with heaven."

"You're leaving?"

"Right away."

"But you can't, you—"

"Five minutes after I leave you won't even remember me. No, no protests. You have each other now. You don't need a nosy old aunt around."

Nellie kissed Berni's cheek. "I will always need you. You are a very kind person." She leaned toward Berni's ear. "I don't know what you did, but I know that last night was your doing. Thank you. I will thank you all my life for your generous heart."

Those words meant a lot to Berni. No one had ever called her generous before, but then she'd never deserved the title before. "Thank you," she whispered, then she straightened. "I must go." She looked at Nellie. "Any wishes for the future?"

"I have everything I want," Nellie said, moving to stand close to Jace.

"I have a wish." Jace looked down at Nellie and remembered his first wife dying in childbirth. "I hope we have a dozen healthy kids and their deliveries are easy on their mother."

"Done," Berni said, then she stood on tiptoe and kissed Jace's cheek. "You'll have all your children, and the deliveries will be safe and easy." She turned and went up the stairs. At the top of the stairs she paused and looked down at them, lovers engrossed in each other. Berni had never done anything that made her feel as good as getting these two together had.

She gave a little sniff, wiped a tear from her eye, and said, "Beam me up, Scotty," and she was gone from the Grayson household and from the Grayson memory.

THE KITCHEN

Pauline was there to greet Berni, and she was smiling.

Berni, once again wearing her burial clothes, took a moment to adjust to the foggy Kitchen after leaving Jace and Nellie. "I did well, didn't I?" she said, pretending she'd never shed a tear at leaving. "You thought I couldn't do it, but I did."

"You did very well," Pauline said, smiling brighter. "You did especially well by not making Nellie hate her family. You could have let her see how selfish they really are."

Berni was a little embarrassed by the praise, even though it felt very good. "There was enough hate and jealousy. I didn't need to spread any more," she mumbled.

"You did very well indeed. Now, shall we go to Level Two?"

Berni's mind was on Nellie. "I guess so." She started walking beside Pauline, then stopped. "Could I see what happened to Nellie? I'd like to be *sure* she did okay."

Pauline gave a little nod and led the way to the Viewing Room. Once they were seated comfortably the screen before them began to clear.

"It's now Christmas 1897," Pauline said, "one year to the day since you left, and Jace and Nellie have been married for a year."

The fog cleared, and Berni could see the Grayson house, decorated for Christmas, and it was filled with people. "Who are they?"

"Jace's relatives came all the way from Maine, and Terel came with her husband, and Charles with his new wife, and then there are the Taggerts from Chandler." Pauline smiled. "Nellie doesn't know it, but she's already carrying her second child. She—"

"Sssh," Berni said, "I want to see for myself."

CHANDLER, COLORADO
Christmas 1897

"When will the new house be finished?" 'Ring Montgomery, Jace's father, asked Charles Grayson, who was sitting at the opposite end of the couch. As he spoke he reached out an arm and caught one of the Tyler boys, who was running through the house at full speed, by the shoulder and gave him a look of warning before releasing him.

"Three more months," Charles shouted above the din. He and his wife were living in Denver until the old Fenton house could be remodeled to his wife's taste. It was costing him every penny he had, but it was worth it to see her happy. He couldn't care less how much he had to spend. "You enjoying Chandler?" he shouted back.

"Very much." 'Ring, unlike Charles, didn't seem in the least bothered by the noise of eleven children and fourteen adults. In one corner of the room Pamela Taggert was loudly playing the piano while Jace and his mother were practicing a Christmas duet for church that evening. "You're flat on that note, son," 'Ring said over the heads of four dirty-faced children.

How in the world he could hear anything Charles didn't know. An hour ago Charles's lovely wife had excused herself and gone upstairs to lie down. Charles wished he could join her.

"Should those children be eating that?" Charles asked.

'Ring looked at the three toddlers in the corner, two of them Kane Taggert's kids, one of them the pig farmer's. "A little dirt never hurt any kid as far as I can tell, but Hank," he said to his twelve-year-old nephew, "see what those kids are eating."

Hank grimaced at having to leave the side of his cousins, eighteen-year-old Zachary and the nearly-adult twenty-one-year-old Ian Taggert. Hank was at the age where he wasn't quite adult and wasn't quite a child. Dutifully, Hank took three bugs from the hands of the toddlers, and all three kids started wailing.

"Take them outside," 'Ring said, making Hank groan.

"What are you two laughin' at?" Kane said to his son Zachary and his cousin, Ian. "Get outside and take care of them kids."

The boys stopped laughing at Hank, and each picked up a child and went outside.

"Now what were you saying?" 'Ring asked Charles.

"The house should be ready in a few months, but—" He broke off at a loud guffaw of laughter from Kane and Rafe Taggert and John Tyler, who were standing together by the foot of the stairs.

"Johnny, honey," Terel said from a corner of the room where she sat lounging on an easy chair, "I believe I'm thirsty. Do fetch me a glass of lemonade."

Charles watched as John Tyler and three of his dirty kids tripped over themselves to go to the kitchen to get Terel whatever she wanted. Terel's marrying a penniless pig farmer had bewildered Charles until he saw them together. The poor, illiterate Tyler family felt honored and privileged to have Terel in their family and treated her as though she were royalty. She lounged about, eating what they cooked for her, wearing what their work paid for, and now and then bestowing a radiant smile upon one of them. It seemed to be enough to satisfy all of them. John and the kids didn't seem to mind that they wore torn, worn-out clothing while Terel dressed exclusively in silk. Charles had seen Terel reward a child by letting him touch her skirt. It didn't make sense to him, but the Tyler family seemed to be quite happy.

Charles gave 'Ring a bit of a smile as if to indicate that further talk was impossible.

"How's that?" Jace called to his father when he'd finished another song.

"Still a little flat on the fourth bar, but better," 'Ring said. He looked at his wife, his eyes, as always, full of love. "You, my dear, were perfection."

Maddie blew him a kiss, then put her music down

on the piano. "I believe my grandchild is crying," she said to her tall, handsome son, nodding to the crib that held two babies, each only a few months old.

"That one's mine," Kane said, and he scooped up a baby and expertly nestled it on his shoulder.

"I think the one you took is mine," Jace said as he picked up the other child, who had also started yelling.

Kane pulled the child from his shoulder and looked down the front of its diaper. His third child was a girl, and this one was a boy. He and Jace exchanged kids.

Maddie laughed, told Pam thanks for playing the piano, and went into the kitchen. Nellie, Houston, and a young girl, Tildy, were up to their elbows in flour and turkey dressing.

"Want to help?" Houston asked, smiling at her husband's cousin's wife.

"Absolutely not," Maddie said, giving a delicate shudder. Maddie had cultivated the image of prima donna for so long that one could almost believe that she'd never seen the inside of a kitchen.

Nellie, looking radiant and as happy as she was, said, "Then you must sing for your supper."

Maddie laughed. It hadn't taken her but minutes to fall in love with her daughter-in-law. "All right. What shall it be? 'Silent Night'? Or something less seasonal?" She took a cookie from a basket and ate it.

Nellie and Houston looked at each other with liquid eyes. A woman with one of the greatest voices of all time was offering to sing just for them, anything they wanted.

Houston took a deep breath. *"Lakmé's* 'Bell Song,'" she whispered, knowing that Delibes's beautiful aria would best show off Maddie's exquisite voice.

Maddie smiled at Houston, then softly said, "Jocelyn, I need you."

Jace put his head into the kitchen, his eyebrows lifted in question to his mother.

"Houston and your wife would like to hear the 'Bell Song.'"

Jace smiled. "Good choice." He looked at his mother. "Where is it?"

"In my bag."

Jace handed his son to his father and within minutes returned with a flute. Nellie watched in wonder as she saw this new aspect of her husband, saw a man who had been surrounded all his life by music. Jace put the flute to his lips and began to play, just enough to accompany his mother's voice.

The "Bell Song," meant to show off the range and variety of a coloratura's voice, began slowly—no words, just a voice, but a voice of such heavenly sweetness that it made one gape in wonder. Maddie's voice played with the notes, trilled them, caressed them as she sang the song, imitating the bells, echoing Jace's high flute notes.

Nellie and Houston stopped working, and the girl Tildy, who had never heard such a voice in her life, stood transfixed.

In the other room everyone grew silent, and even the babies stopped crying as Maddie played with each note, holding it, loving it, until her listeners had tears of joy in their eyes.

When she finished there wasn't a sound in the house until one of the pig-dirty Tyler kids, gaping at the back door, said, "Damnation, ain't never heard nothin' like that afore."

With that, everyone broke into laughter, and all the adults, kids over shoulders, tucked under arms, held by the hand, crowded into the kitchen.

"Exquisite," 'Ring said, pulling his wife into his arms. "I've never heard you sing better."

"It's the influence of the love in this house," she whispered against his lips.

They all stood around the table that was heaped with food, each husband holding his wife.

"Is that what's making me so happy?" Jace asked Nellie, pulling her close with one arm, his baby son in the other. "All the love in this house?"

"Yes," Nellie said, tears in her eyes. "I never thought I'd know this much love or be this happy. I didn't know this much happiness existed."

Jace kissed her.

"Here!" Kane said loudly. "If we're all so happy, how come everybody's cryin'? Maddie, you know any *real* songs? How about 'Half a Penny, Half a Bushel'? Or 'Ring Tailed Ringating'?"

"Kane," Houston said firmly, "I doubt very much if someone of Maddie's caliber knows—" She broke off as Maddie burst into a rousing song worthy of any saloon singer and, laughing, everyone began to sing with her.

"She ain't a bad singer after all," Kane said to his wife.

Nellie, singing along, looked at her husband holding their child, then at the other people around her. It was still disconcerting to see her immaculately groomed sister snuggled up to her perpetually dirty husband, but Terel seemed to adore him, and the children as well. Nellie looked at her father, his arm around his plump wife who had just joined everyone. Her ears sparkled with the diamond earrings he'd given her for Christmas, and Nellie knew that her dress bill for this month alone made Terel's former expenses seem nonexistent. But again, she'd never seen her father so happy.

Nellie squeezed Jace's hand and moved closer to his side. "I am the happiest person on earth," she said softly, and he kissed her again.

THE KITCHEN

Berni sniffed, then gave Pauline an embarrassed look. "I'm very happy for her. She deserves to have some good things happen to her."

"You made everyone happy," Pauline said, standing and leaving the room.

"I guess I did," Berni said proudly as she followed her. "Although I meant for Terel to learn a little humility."

"You didn't really think she'd wash and iron, did you? Would *you* have?"

"Not on your life!"

They looked at each other and laughed.

"Okay," Berni said, "so now I go to Heaven, right?"

"Not quite."

"But I thought—"

"You really haven't paid your dues yet."

"Dues for what?"

"You haven't paid your dues for living a completely selfish life on earth."

"I helped Nellie."

"Yes, you did. That was stage one, and you passed very, very well, but still you need to experience some of the things that other women experienced while they were on earth."

"Such as?" Berni asked suspiciously. "I don't have to become one of those athletic women, do I? Run? Climb mountains, that sort of thing?"

"No, nothing like that, just ordinary woman things."

Berni wasn't sure what she meant. It seemed to her she'd experienced everything a woman could while on earth. What else was there? "What are you talking about?"

Pauline stopped and looked at her, her face serious. "There's something I think I'd better explain. There are levels to the Kitchen. Some of them are pleasant, but some of them are . . . not so pleasant. Level One, which you've been to, is to introduce you to the

Kitchen and to cushion the blow of death. Level Two is . . ."

"Is what?" Berni asked.

"Level Two makes you very concerned about doing your job well—your earthly job, that is."

"You mean I'm to be somebody else's fairy god-mother?" She thought a moment. "It wasn't so bad. It was kinda fun, actually."

"I'm glad you think so, because you must do it again—only the second time there is a bit more urgency."

"You mean there's a time limit?"

"No, not exactly. It's just that most people are somewhat anxious to leave Level Two."

The fog before them cleared, and Berni could see a sign. "Just as before," Pauline said, "you must choose one room in which to wait."

As they moved forward Berni could read the sign. "No," she whispered, abruptly turning away.

Pauline caught her. "You must choose."

"I can't." Berni buried her face in her hands. "They're all too horrible. Couldn't I just go to hell and be burned alive for eternity?"

"I'm afraid that's the easy way out. You didn't earn heaven while you were on earth, so now you must suffer as other women have suffered." Pauline turned Berni around and made her look at the sign. "You must choose."

Berni forced herself to open her eyes and look at the sign once again.

WISHES

1. a trip across America in a sports car with three kids and a dog
2. backpacking and sleeping in a tent with your stepchildren
3. TV that runs only PBS pledge drive twenty-four hours a day
4. clothes shopping with a man

"Clothes shopping with a man?" Berni whispered in horror.

"It's more horrible than you can believe," Pauline said. "Before you leave the house he makes you tell him exactly what you want to buy, what color, what style, what fabric. In the store he folds his arms and glares at you and looks at his watch. Sometimes you have to shop with him for his own purchases. You search two hundred and seventy-one stores for exactly the pair of shoes he wants, you finally find them, and he says the stitches on the toe are one thirty-second of an inch too long."

Berni's face lost all color as she looked back at the sign.

5. dieting while raising three teenage daughters
6. at home with eight sick kids—or one sick husband
7. driving a car with a male passenger who keeps screaming and whimpering
8. trapped in an elevator with your husband's ex-wife

9. a husband who retires and wants you to spend every minute with him

10. a boss who constantly makes passes at you

"No," Berni kept whispering, but she knew she had no choice. She raised a trembling hand and pointed. "Just get me out of here quick," she said to Pauline before the fog cleared away from the horror she had chosen.

The Duchess

Jude Deveraux

Claire Willoughby, a beautiful young American heiress, had been trained her whole life for one thing— to be an English duchess. But when she travels to Scotland to visit her fiance, Harry Montgomery, the duke of McArran, she finds out his family is more than she'd bargained for. Fascinated by his peculiar family, Claire is most intrigued by Trevelyan Montgomery, Harry's mysterious brilliant cousin who she finds living secretly in an unused part of the estate. As she spends more and more time with the magnetic Trevelyan, Claire finds herself drawn to him against her will, yearning to know everything about him. But if Trevelyan's secret is discovered life at Bramley will never be the same.

COMING IN HARDCOVER
FROM POCKET BOOKS
IN FALL 1991

POCKET
B O O K S

Jude Deveraux

A Unique New Voice In Romantic Fiction

Jude Deveraux is the finest new writer of historical romances to come along since Kathleen Woodiwiss.

The Montgomery Annals